The Stuyvesant Connection

Tom Riley

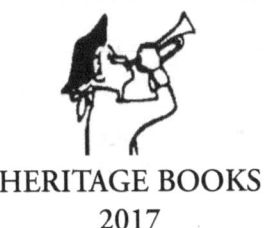

HERITAGE BOOKS
2017

HERITAGE BOOKS

AN IMPRINT OF HERITAGE BOOKS, INC.

Books, CDs, and more—Worldwide

For our listing of thousands of titles see our website
at
www.HeritageBooks.com

Published 2017 by
HERITAGE BOOKS, INC.
Publishing Division
5810 Ruatan Street
Berwyn Heights, Md. 20740

International Standard Book Numbers
Paperbound: 978-0-7884-5753-1

CHAPTER I

Michael Ryan snaked away from the tangle of bodies wrestling on the old double bed. He found safety at the edge nearest the wall. He laughed to himself as he lay with his back pressed tightly against the wall. He cradled his head with the palm of his right hand as he watched Patrick slip from the bottom of the tangled mass, edge off the bed, and slowly back away.

He laughed again as Patrick picked up forward momentum, leaped with arms extended, and crashed with a fleshly thud on the three brothers below. The big, old rickety bed slammed against the wall. Michael rode out the shock and repositioned himself.

Looking down on the blue-lined mattress he focused his eyes on two skittering bed-bugs racing away from the volcanic forces rocking the old bed. A loud yelp of pain broke his revelry as one of the combatants started to cry.

"Cool it, you guys, you'll wake the old man!" Michael said. Michael peered under the shaded French doors and saw the slumbering figure of his father tossing restlessly and uttering mumbled curses in his sleep. A cherry-stained night stand held a can of Ballantine beer and a plastic musician's flute. At the foot of the bed Michael could see his father's red tool box. It hadn't been open in two and a half years, ever since his father had been laid off from the Brooklyn Navy Yard.

Now the family subsisted from day to day on meager welfare payments and on the catfish and eels, caught by a father who seemingly had found his true vocation on the peer off 125th street. There, men with plenty of time on their hands idly soaked up the sun and drank beer as they waited for blue-fin crabs to be lured into their metal traps. The rapid disappearance of numerous bobbers signaled a lucky catch of eels, flounder and sometimes codfish.

The smell of machine oil, fish, urine, and unchanged bedding gave the apartment a distinctive odor. The machine oil was used to keep his father's reels in good working order. The fish smell arose from the bathroom where eels, flounder and crabs happily co-existed until one of his brothers mischievously turned on the hot water. Then the smell of dead marine life cause a rapid evacuation of the apartment until his poor mother cleaned out the tub.

Michael heard his mother admonish the boys not to wake their father. Her voice was tired and pained and hardly heard above the din.

"Cool it you guys! We're going to catch hell if the old man wakes up." said Michael in a concerned voice.

Kevin grabbed Michael by the foot. The other three joined in and pulled Michael into the pile. Patrick again slid off the bed and repeated his flying leap: This time the wooden struts supporting the sides of the bed gave way with a loud bang against the linoleum floor. The headboard and baseboard collapsed inward. The startled boys laughed nervously, stared at each other, then raced for position pretending to be asleep on the collapsed mattress. Michael lifted the headboard away from the mattress and buttressed it against the wall. He grabbed a blanket and flared it about his four sleeping brothers feigning a deep sleep.

In the other room, he heard his father yell with rage at the commotion in the next room. Michael saw his father grab the curled belt that lay in readiness on the night table. He knocked over the half-filled beer can and cursed. "You lousy kids are really gonna get it now!"

Staggering to his feet, he knocked over the night stand and cursed abusively.

"Shush kids, your father is up and raving mad" said a pitiful voice from the kitchen.

"The old man is coming! Cool it, you guys," Michael yelled.

Michael saw the pane-glass door begin to open. He pretended to snore tranquilly. Out of the corner of his eye he saw the raging toothless man as he stood above the cowering, blanketed boys. Fear paralyzed him as he saw the dark shadow of a belt as it whipped through the air and snapped across his face. He screamed in agony as he felt a knife-like pain above his left eye. His brothers shot from under the blanket. He saw his frightened mother run from the kitchen and grab the belt from his staggering father.

"Stop it, Liam! Look what you did to his face."

"Gimme that belt, woman!" He saw his mother retreat into the kitchen and a wild look on his father's face.

It was a fearful and crazy world. Michael felt the blows and silently pondered their meaning. Life was threatened daily. The unexpected erupted regularly. His brothers and he were forced participants in a ritual of degradation and poverty. Michael rubbed his beating chest and felt the sharply-defined bones radiating from it. Each finger fell into the grooves of his ribs and followed an upward curving symmetry toward his protruding sternum.

Michael felt the ominous presence of his father as he stood above him.

"You can forget about that trip to Kentucky, 'cause you ain't going. You hear me?" he said pointing at Michael. "Tell them your mother is sick and needs an operation and that you'll take the money instead."

"Why? So, you can spend it on the horses or go to Florida like you did before." Michael said defiantly.

"Don't get smart with me. You know I didn't mean to hit ya. You kids woke me from a bad dream with your racket." His father rubbed his stubbled face and retreated to his room closing the pane-glass door behind him.

Michael walked to a small room off the hallway leading to the entrance of the apartment. A simulated desk had been constructed from a piece of wallboard and two orange crates. The orange crates were filled with books and magazines crammed with articles and information about the desalinization of water as a solution to the problem of hunger and the encroaching deserts that were threatening Africa and other parts of the world.

THE STUYVESANT CONNECTION

From between a book he pulled out a certified letter announcing that he had been picked a co-winner in a science essay. He remembered all the work he had put into it. The project had grown from a small beginning but had become a labor of love the more he worked on it. He and his closest friend, Bernard had challenged each other to produce a science project that could win. Michael's project on desalinization had led him to research material on the largest such plant that was located in the Saudi Arabian Peninsula. He was amazed at the social, economic and political implications such a project was having on the whole area.

Using the success this one plant was having, he wrote an essay superimposing the possibilities on other areas of the world facing drought and the encroaching desert. It was a complete and thorough report over thirty pages long and filled with graphs, diagrams, and illustrations. His total involvement with his science project had distracted him from the growing problems at home.

Mike's friend Bernard had chosen the subject of meteorites. Michael remembered the day they submitted their entries to Mr. Rubin, the guidance counsellor at Stuyvesant High School. Walking out of his office, they had smacked their palms together and raised their hand in a victory salute, believing for the first time they had a chance of winning.

Michael kissed the letter, carefully folded it and placed it deep inside a dictionary so that his father couldn't find it and act on his own. Returning the book to his makeshift desk, he saw a cat slowly and silently stalking what appeared to be a white pigeon feeding on garbage that had been thrown in the courtyard five stories below. Moving closer to the window he saw the cat leap upon the pigeon, but like a phoenix the bird rose from the courtyard below. He followed its flight as it soared above him and cleared the tenement roof heading for the river, three blocks west.

Buttoning his shirt, he entered the kitchen and walked over to his mother, placing a hand on her shoulder. She didn't look up.

THE STUYVESANT CONNECTION

"I'm going to make that trip to Kentucky and he's not going to stop me."

She turned and lightly caressed the welt above his left eye. "Put some ice on that before you leave for school. I want you to take that trip. It will be good for you to get away from here."

Michael saw tears well up in her eyes. He squeezed her shoulders and tried to comfort her. The smell of urine, machine oil, and fish returned to him. The wall clock pointed at 8am. He had to go and see Bernard and talk about their decision. As he passed the bathroom, a catfish made an abrupt turn in the tub spilling water on the floor.

CHAPTER II

Bernard Jones heard the alarm go off but tried to shut it out of his mind. Ten minutes later his mother called out from the next room.

"OK Ma, I'm coming," he said as he rolled to the right side of the bed, eyes still closed, and grasped about the night table for his glasses.

"Specs, specs, where are you," he murmured to himself, thinking, darn my eyes are getting bad. I hope they never get as bad as Dad's. He's almost blind. He can hardly see the typeset at the printers. No sir, I'm never going to let that happen to me. I'm gonna keep my health and still get rich. Only fools hurt themselves. No job is worth hurtin' your health.

Bernard rolled out of bed and cautiously approached the bureau several feet away. Astigmatism, a hereditary trait on his father's side made life a blur without his thick spectacles. He felt about until he found his glasses atop a book on rock climbing. Putting them on, he saw a large poster of Mean Joe Greene come into view. His finger pointed directly at Bernard and said, "TEAM UP WITH YOUR TEACHER."

Oh no, Bernard thought to himself. I forgot to do my geometry homework. I hope Mike comes over. I still got time to copy his. I'm tired of Mr. Thomas calling my Mom. Lucky science is my ace. Ever since I won that Science Essay they haven't call my Mom. I gotta laugh — everybody turned their head in disbelief when they announced me as a co-winner.

Bernard opened the closet door and considered his options. Let's see...what am I going to wear today? That tan pullover will look good with my Easy Striders. I hope they cancel gym today 'cause somebody stole my Pro-Keds. I wonder who did? Reggie Doaks! I just remembered. He was eyeing my Keds on Tuesday. Made some crack about them being just his size. I'm gonna check him out today. He'd steal from his own brother. Doaks is gonna get poked if he fled with my Keds.

His mother called out for him once more.

"Yea, Ma, I'll be right there. I'm coming."

I wonder what's for breakfast. Bacon and eggs, I hope. Mom has been forgetting my favorites lately. All she has on her mind is getting that promotion at the factory. Eight twenty, gotta get moving. Hope Mike gets here soon.

The doorbell interrupted his reveries. He heard his mother greet Mike and tell him to get Bernard moving. "Hey, Mike! What's happening? Listen, can I borrow your geometry assignment. It's due today and I completely forgot about it until this morning. We still got twenty minutes."

Mike opened his loose-leaf binder and handed two pages to his friend. Bernard sat at a small desk and hurriedly copied the assignment.

"Where'd you get that shiner, Mike?"

"My old man gave me a wallop for waking him from a bad dream."

Bernard looked at his friend's face. The welt over his eye had come close to being an open wound. Bernard felt sorry that Mike seemed to be a target for his father's frustrations. It wasn't the first time Mike had taken a beating. He found himself somewhat amused at his feelings of pity for a white boy, but caught himself because Mike and he were solid. It was Mike who had encouraged him to enter the science essay. They had spent more time in the library the last three months than they did on the basketball court.

"He's been losing his temper quite a bit lately, huh, Mike? You gotta get out of that scene, Mike," Bernard said as he hurriedly scribbled away.

"Bernie, you're going on that trip to Mammoth with me, right?"

"I don't know, Mike. You know it's right during the finals of the basketball tournament. I don't want to miss that. You shouldn't either; it took us three years to have a winning season. I think I'll ask Mr. Rubin if I can pass up the trip and only accept the $250.00 cash award."

"You sound like my father. He wants me to take the money and run. You can't do that, Bernie. It's all or nothing. If you refuse the trip, they'll pick another entry. And you need this award for your files. You were treading on thin ice before this thing. It was only three weeks ago, that Mr. Rubin said you should consider another school, remember? This is the best thing to happen to you since you came to Stuyvesant."

"Yea, I guess you're right. My mom and dad can't believe I won that science essay. She hasn't received a call from Mr. Thomas in two weeks. It's like it has a carryover effect on the other teachers."

Bernard thought about the work he had done on his winning entry. He had chosen the subject of meteorites after seeing one of the largest in the world at the Museum of Natural History. It had landed in Greenland over 10,000 years ago. The Eskimos of Greenland worshipped it as a deity and for centuries had chipped pieces off it to make spears and arrowheads of the iron-ore mixture.

In his report, Bernard advanced the latest theory by the father-son team of scientists named Alvarez who discovered that a thin layer of globally distributed clay between strata of the Cretaceous and Tertiary periods was rich in the element iridium. They believe this iridium was fallout from the life extinguishing impact of meteorites and that it ended the age of dinosaurs

"You could practice some of your rock climbing techniques when we have that day of wild caving that they promised on the tour. It's going to be a real adventure, Bernard, crawling through passages with only kerosene lamps to guide us. They want you to experience what it was like when the cave system was first discovered," Michael said.

"Yea, Mike, that sounds like fun. I'd get a chance to use some rock climbing techniques I've been working on at Eagle Rock."

THE STUYVESANT CONNECTION

Bernard finished copying the assignment and handed it back to Mike.

"Let me show you a tune I composed on the piano. It's called "Chelsea Blues," Bernard said in an effort to change the subject. With very little training Bernard had developed a knack for picking up various melodies and transforming them into piano pieces. Bernard pecked away at the family piano until Mike could recognize something coming out of the experimentation.

"It's pretty good but needs a latta work," said Mike. Hey, Bernie, we gotta get going." "Wait, let me grab some grits. You want a fried egg sandwich or something?"

"No, Bernie, we don't have much time left."

Bernard finished breakfast while Mrs. Jones fixed a hot cup of chocolate for Mike. She gave a cup to her son and held his face in a fond gesture.

"My son, the scientist! You made me and Leroy so proud. Bernard pushed away from the table. "Come on, Ma, I'm spilling my orange juice."

She looked at Mike and asked about his injury.

Bernard saw Mike's eyes cloud over as he told her he had been wrestling with his brothers and bumped his head on a table.

"Time to go," said Bernard as he gathered his books.

He blew a kiss to his mother and hurriedly left the apartment bounding down the steps with Michael two at a time. Stepping out into the bright sunshine Bernard spied a bagel under the bakery truck adjacent to the entrance of his apartment building.

"Hey, Mike, what's that bagel doing under that truck?" Reaching down he picked it up and tossed it to a man coming out of the bakery.

"Hey, Wags-you dropped your breakfast."

Bernard broke into a run as the black man one-handed the tossed bagel and feigned an advance toward the two boys. Bernard knew Wags had a good sense of humor. For years, they had been feigning antagonism toward each other and today's prank made him laugh.

The two boys took the A train to 42nd street and then switched to the cross-town local to catch the downtown local. They exited the subway station and headed in the direction of Stuyvesant High School.

"Hey, Mike, isn't that Doaks up ahead? Now he's got some nerve. Look, he wearing my Keds. He must have taken them from my locker when my back was turned. Let's burn some rubber and catch that brother. He's gonna be walking around with a bruise for a head. It'll serve him right for stealing my Keds. What a fool wearing my Keds to school. With my shoes on his feet he's trying to look neat, but when I burn rubber, he's in for a treat."

Michael pulled him from behind and brought him to a stop. "Bernie, he has three guys with him. Use your head. There's no way you can take those sneakers off him."

"I don't care! They belong to me. My mother put my name in them. Well here goes," said Bernard with a forced bravado. The closer he approached Doaks, the more he began to make a more realistic appraisal of the situation.

"Hey, Doaks, those Keds you're wearing sure look neat. Are you sure you've got them on the right feet?" said Bernard as fear made his voice change to a higher pitch

Reggie Doaks looked at them in disbelief. He looked at his three friends then he said, "Bernard, those glasses you're wearing — are you sure they're all right? You accuse me of stealing — they might break in a fight." With that he grabbed Bernard by the shoulder and shook him.

Bernard broke free and took off with Michael alongside of him. Rounding a corner, he said to his friend, "My mother would kill me if I broke my glasses. I think I'll let him go for now. Bunch of dummies, too. Doaks will be transferring next week. Good riddance!"

THE STUYVESANT CONNECTION

Wow! That was close, thought Bernard. Doaks could have those sneakers. Those three dudes with him looked like they were spoiling for a fight. Gotta make sure I avoid him in the hallway today, he thought.

THE STUYVESANT CONNECTION

CHAPTER III

Tran Lok and Lydia Velez were making their way up the steps to the venerable high school called Stuyvesant. For years, it had nourished the intellectual capacities of New York City's best and brightest students. Tran felt a great sense of pride in attending Stuyvesant. He had been in the U.S. six years now and to be accepted into one of its finest high schools was to keep faith with his mother and father.

Tran was a refugee of the Communist takeover in Cambodia. He was the only member of his family to get out of Cambodia. He had heard nothing from his parents since the day he left· Cambodia. Left? Carried out was more like it.

His father had run a small store and was able to get Tran out of his village before it came under siege. His mother had given him a gold pocket watch that belonged to his grandfather and had accompanied him to Phnom Penh. She tearfully kissed him goodbye and instructed him to make it to the gates of the American Embassy, to tell them that his grandfather had been a U.S. citizen.

Phnom Penh was under siege. He was nearly trampled to death when he fell under the crush of people trying to get into the embassy. An American Marine, seeing his plight, clubbed away at the throng, picked up Tran's nearly lifeless body, and passed him to another marine inside the embassy.

He awoke in an American hospital in the Philippines. After a short stay in a refugee camp he had been adopted by an American geologist who had spent several years in Asia working for an oil company. His American mother was a school teacher. She helped Tran excel in his classwork. He had some difficulty with English but showed great aptitude in science. His entry on the use of laser technology in producing holographic images showed a remarkable understanding of physics.

THE STUYVESANT CONNECTION

Lydia had helped him by proofreading his entry and smoothing out the phrasing. He had befriended the pretty, shy Hispanic girl in the math class they shared. She seemed ill at ease; her shyness made it difficult to engage in small talk. Tran had experienced these feelings too. The two easily became friends. Tran helped her with geometry, a subject she was having difficulty in. He learned that she was a resident of St. Thaddeus, a home for neglected young people and those in need of supervision.

Tran turned around when he heard his name called. Michael and Bernard bounded up the steps.

"Hi, Michael, Bernie. What happened to your eye, Michael? Did you get into a fight?" asked Tran.

Michael touched the area and seemed to want to change the subject. "What time are we supposed to meet with Mr. Rubin to talk over the itinerary of the trip, Tran?" Michael asked.

Bernard commented on how good Lydia looked in her pink sweater. Her long black hair cascaded about her shoulders. Holding her books against her full figure she smiled and nervously thanked Bernard for the compliment.

"You guys practicing for a race or something, the way you were running?" asked Tran, as he noticed the beads of perspiration on their foreheads.

"No, we were just taking care of business," said Bernard with a wink to Mike.

"Yea, it's a matter Bernie is going to clear up." Michael winked back.

"Let's go, people. It's almost nine and the late bell is going to ring," said Tran as the four ascended the steps together. "We'll meet in the cafeteria," he added as the big oak doors closed behind them.

At 12:15 pm Tran stood in line as hundreds of hungry mouths glanced at the trays passing to their left. "Oh yes!" and "Not again," could be heard through the cacophony of silverware, conversation, and sliding tables and chairs. Tran whistled as he saw Lydia, Mike and Bernard. He motioned that he would reserve a table for them. At

16

THE STUYVESANT CONNECTION

12:30 the four were seated together and spoke above the rising din and myriad apples and oranges undergoing airborne exchange.

"Mr. Rubin said we're to meet him at 2 pm in the guidance office," Tran said as he brushed away an errant straw cover launched in his direction by Bernie.

"Oh good, that's my geometry class. It gives me a chance to finish my homework," Bernard said as he ripped the cellophane from an apple Danish. Bernard told the group how incredulous his parents were when they learned he had won the science essay. His father had taken the letter to work to show his co-workers. His mother was still beaming over his accomplishments.

Tran saw a momentary trace of sadness come over Michael's face at Bernard's affectionate description of his parents' reaction. When Tran asked Michael about his parents' reaction, Michael leaned away from the table and said, "My old man doesn't want me to go. He'd rather I take the money and run, But I'm looking forward to the trip. How about you, Tran?"

"My father is a geologist and has been filling me in on cave geology. It's a great chance to see another part of the country. Winning a science essay looks good on your resume. It sure should help me to get into M.I.T. I want to be a physicist but my father enjoys geology and feels such a trip could really turn me on to geology."

As the others talked about what they would bring to Kentucky, Tran reflected on his good fortune. His real father's admonition to get a good education was becoming a reality. He thought about the months that followed his departure from Cambodia. He and thousands of other refugees had been quartered in old wooden barracks in the Philippines. There they were well-fed and treated for the wounds and infections incurred on a refugee's journey. He found the Americans to be big-hearted and generous hosts. They seemed to comprise people from every race: white, black, oriental, Jews, Christians, Arabs, and atheists. He had met them all in his six-

17

month-stay at the camp. They taught English daily. For many it was very difficult.

One day he saw a man changing a light bulb in his barracks. He had retrieved a ladder from a utility closet. Tran was determined to overcome his difficulty with English. Every night while others slept, he would perch himself atop the ladder, placed his gold watch nearby, and study his English workbook from the red glow of the exit sign. At 3 am he would climb down from his perch, store the ladder away and go to sleep. The other refugees would call him "glowworm" for his nocturnal study habits. His progress in English was rapid and amazed his teachers.

The cafeteria bell rang signaling the beginning of afternoon classes. Tran gathered his books together, emptied his tray, and told his friends he would meet them at 2 pm in Mr. Rubin's office. In two minutes the clamorous din of the cafeteria fell silent as the students made their way to afternoon classes.

THE STUYVESANT CONNECTION

CHAPTER IV

Lydia Velez sat in the homeroom and thought about the events of the past year. So much had happened; incredible changes had taken place. She felt grateful for all the good things that had occurred. A year ago, the Family Court in Brooklyn had remanded her to St. Thaddeus, a home for young people in need of supervision and guidance. She thought about her mother — her father had died five years ago.

Her mother, so badly riddled with arthritis was unable to work at her job as a maid. Things had gotten steadily worse. Lydia began to hang out with friends who were into smoking pot and petty shoplifting. Lydia had seen what alcohol did to her father and had no desire to become dependent on marijuana.

When one of her friends lent her a beautiful leather jacket she didn't know that it had been stolen from Bambergers. An investigation into her home situation and Mrs. Velez's illness caused her social worker to recommend placement into child care. Lydia and her mother had been receiving welfare for years. Her mother was sent to a rehabilitation facility in Westchester for three months.

At first Lydia had rebelled against the structure and seemingly mean counsellors. Her social worker recognized her intelligence and confirmed it with an I.Q. test. Her social worker, Mrs. Trentacoste had been a graduate of Stuyvesant and was determined that Lydia would have an opportunity to challenge her intellect. The first six months at Stuyvesant were difficult. The amount of homework demanded from her caused her to rebel against its academic standards. Then along came the essay contest on science her first love.

Gradually the stability St. Thaddeus offered, and the chance to immerse herself in an all-consuming project under the steady encouragement of Mrs. Trentacoste, led her all the way to the present moment — new friends, opportunity to travel, and the respect of her peers for academic excellence. Her essay dealt with the Theory of Plate Tectonics. It was a labor of love and discovery. She had included maps, graphs, and a scale model of the earth's molten core constructed from different colors of clay laid over a sliding plastic globe. It had been possible to demonstrate the phenomena and destruction caused by the movement of the earth's plates. It was the first time she ever received an award. The fact that it involved a monetary award and travel made her feel like a celebrity.

The bell rang. Lydia brushed back her hair using her fingers as a comb. Gathering her books together she joined two of her classmates on her way to her afternoon class. A smile came to her face as her friends excitedly asked about her award. It was a knowing smile based on a new knowledge of effort and achievement and reflected her gratitude. One of the girls remarked how proud Lydia's mom must be of her achievement.

Lydia became thoughtful and serious as she recalled the events of last Saturday. She remembered her mother's reaction when she told her about the award. She had requested a pass to see her mother for the weekend. She got off the subway train and had walked through her old neighborhood. Debris and litter filled the streets. Men huddled around barrels with fires in them at street corners. Wine bottles and whiskey flasks peeked from overcoat pockets. As she entered a shabby building, several men scurried from the foyer. A syringe and several bottle tops lay on the floor. She trudged up four flights to 4B. Hesitantly, she knocked on the door.

"Who's there?"

"Lydia."

"Lydia, what are you doing away from the home?"

"Ma, I got a pass until Sunday and I have some good news."

Lydia heard another voice in the apartment. When her mother opened the door and embraced her, Lydia saw a man in the background. He held a cigarette and was nervously flicking the ashes into the cup of his other hand.

"Ma, I'm going to stay overnight. I should have phoned but I wanted to tell you the good news in person."

"Lydia, I love you baby, but you can't stay here. Carlos lives with me now and there is only one bed.

Carlos, this is my daughter, Lydia."

Carlos was a slightly stooped Hispanic man wearing a white tee shirt. Nicotine-stained fingers were visible on the hand that held the cigarette. Carlos bowed slightly. He smiled, showing gold capped teeth.

"Ma, I won a science contest. We're going to Kentucky for a week to explore caves."

"That's nice Lydia, but what can I do? Carlos has to work the night shift. He should be resting now. Wait! I'll make a bed for you on the floor."

"No, Ma." A sudden sadness overwhelmed her. She turned toward the door.

"I think I'll take a walk."

"Lydia, I love you."

"I know, Ma."

Tears filled her eyes as she closed the door behind her. She knew what she had to do. She had to go home and see Mrs. Trent and share her award and joy with her. She knew Mrs. Trent would appreciate the magnitude of her accomplishment and fuss over her achievement.

At 2 pm she joined Tran, Mike, and Bernie in Mr. Rubin's office. Mr. Rubin was a tall, thin man with wavy black hair and horn-rimmed glasses. He greeted each student with a warm handshake and personal congratulations.

"It's not often that Stuyvesant High School fields four winners in The Citibank Science Essay. We've always had a winner but having four winners is a bumper crop for us. First, I want to say how proud we are of you. You competed against 4,000 students.

THE STUYVESANT CONNECTION

Your essays are going to be entered in the prestigious Westinghouse Science Fair so there is the possibility of further awards."

Lydia looked about the office. Plants lined the triple windows while posters and photographs filled the spaces around the room. Letters from former students were neatly framed, all bearing the letterheads of well-known colleges and universities.

"A formal presentation will take place during assembly on Friday. At that time, Mr. Reynolds, the chairman of Citibank will formally present you with your awards. You will be receiving a plaque and a check for $250.00 each. Your week-long trip to Kentucky will be all expenses paid and will begin April 8th. I assume you all will be going?" He looked around at each student. Bernard was scribbling away at his geometry homework.

"Any problem going, Bernard?"

Bernard looked up, closed his notebook. "No problem at all, Mr. Rubin."

"Good," Reaching into his desk he pulled out four manila envelopes and handed them to Lydia to pass around. "You'll be traveling to Kentucky without an escort. You'll be met in Lexington, Kentucky as soon as you get off the train by Todd Green. He will be your constant companion all the time you are in Kentucky. Everything you need is spelled out in your folder. Any questions? Do me a favor, will you? Don't go wandering off. Stay together. That whole area down there is like a giant piece of Swiss cheese, riddled with passages. We want our top students back in time for the Westinghouse Science Fair in May."

"Right, Bernard?"

Bernard stopped writing and took the proffered envelope. "You bet! Mr. Rubin."

"Again congratulations, Stuyvesant is proud of you. Have a safe trip, take plenty of pictures and watch out for each other."

THE STUYVESANT CONNECTION

CHAPTER V

Michael quietly slipped out of the apartment while his brothers slept. He had said goodbye to his mother and brothers hours earlier. He gave $100.00 to his mother for groceries from his prize money, happy knowing that they would eat well for at least two weeks. Closing the door behind him he felt like a thief in the night or more like that pigeon he had seen escaping the pouncing cat. He knew that he would have to face his raging father again but for at least a week he had the freedom to explore new ground, rather underground. He had rescued an old straw suitcase that had been abandoned in the boiler room of his building: the corners were frayed but the lock held and it did the job.

Cautiously he made his way down two landings where light bulbs had been taken by tenants. It was also a common tactic of muggers to lure innocent tenants into unlit landings, then appropriate their valuables. Once into better lighting he bounded down the steps, passed through a darkened hallway and exited through the vestibule door. A cool breeze replaced the fetid air of the hallways.

Except for a few cars that roared up Amsterdam Avenue and the flickering neon signs of all night bars, the streets were deserted. Michael made his way to the elevated subway at 125th Street. He was to meet Bernard, Lydia and Tran at 8:30 am in front of Penn Station. They were all going to breakfast at McDonalds before boarding the *Silver Chief* to Louisville, Kentucky, a twenty-hour train ride. This was his first trip outside of New York City.

Images of Kentucky passed through his mind, The Kentucky Derby, horses, bluegrass and Stephen Foster's Old Kentucky Home. Now he was going under that Kentucky ground to explore some of the more than 300 miles of underground passages, rivers, and great halls. Climbing the elevated steps to the overhead subway station, he entered the Seventh Avenue local. He sat across from two young

27

men sprawled sound asleep on the long subway bench. Obviously having drunk too much, they would remain passed out until a T.A. cop woke them or ordered them off the train. As the train slowed to a stop at Columbia University, Michael saw that it was 6:30 am on the station clock.

Columbia University had a special meaning to Michael. Two years ago, he had met two of the nicest people he had ever known. They were students at the university and very much in love. The man played a guitar and they sang folk songs to Michael and his brothers that cast a spell over Michael — songs full of love and intelligence. Michael associated them with Columbia University and vowed that someday he would go to this school.

Michael got off 59th Street. He decided he would walk the 25 blocks to Penn Station. Dawn cut through the inky darkness as yellow cabs roared around Columbus Circle and raced up Central Park West carrying night time revelers to their lairs for a good day's rest. The sun filtered through the cross-town street. It was going to be a beautiful day.

As he walked down 8th Ave, several young women stared intently, then winked and beckoned him into the foyer of rundown tenements. Michael laughed to himself for being mistaken for an out-of-towner. A walk down 8th Avenue through midtown was always an adventure filled with a tinge of danger for a young man.

He stopped at a coffee shop near the theatre district. The city was awake and bustling with activity. Across the street theater personnel were replacing lights in the marquee for "The Mystery of Edwin Drood." Michael ordered a cup of coffee. He checked his wallet; he had never felt so rich and free. He had $150.00 left over from the prize money. He checked the wall clock. It was only 7:30 am. He still had a full hour before he would meet Bernie, Tran and Lydia. The coffee shop began to fill with drivers for *The New York Times*, theater maintenance personnel, and night people with haggard, tired eyes who had finished their night tours and were on their way home.

THE STUYVESANT CONNECTION

Picking up his frayed suitcase, he paid the bill and headed for Penn Station, twelve blocks away. At 38th Street he cut over to 7th Avenue and dodged clothing racks being pushed by burly men through the darting crowd. As he neared Penn Station, he looked for a sign of his friends. He made out the figure of Lydia reading the digital display announcing the events at Madison Square Garden. From a distance, she looked statuesque in tight fitting jeans and a white, woolen sweater. Her black hair cascaded over her shoulders. She had two pieces of luggage, one a large suitcase, the other a miniature duffel bag hung from her shoulder.

"Lydia, Hi! Where's Bernard and Tran?"

"Tran and Bernard are across the street doing some last-minute shopping for supplies they think they'll need. Did you bring everything you think you'll need?" she asked looking at the frayed suitcase.

"I brought books, a couple of lanterns, some warm clothes, a few snacks, a pair of Reeboks and guess what I got for each of us?"

"What?"

"Four Mets batting helmets. My brothers and I went with the P.A.L. to a Mets game. It was Helmet Day. I figured they'd come in handy when we got a chance to do two days of wild caving. Hate to lose a friend to falling rocks. The books all have to do with the Mammoth Cave System. The best one is *The Longest Cave*. It's fantastic."

Mike saw Tran and Bernie as they dodged the 7th Avenue traffic to join them. Bernard looked like a mountaineer. He had a hundred foot length of half inch nylon rope slung over his shoulder and he wore a bright orange parka with numerous pockets. Tran and Bernie both had mountaineering knapsacks mounted on aluminum frames. Each knapsack had several compartments that could be separated and carried individually. The aluminum frame placed horizontally could be pulled as a sled if needed. Tran wore a lightly-padded nylon jacket with rugged denim parachute pants. A pair of safety glasses from his breast pocket; he held them up to his eyes and looked into the morning sun. "What do you think, Mike? I also got a week's supply of freeze dried food just in case we need it. We're ready for anything."

"You guys look like you're ready to do some serious cave exploration. You know it's really a guided tour we're going on. The two days of wild caving comes at the end and even that's with a guide."

"Mike, you gotta be ready for anything. When we get some time, I want to show you some knots and rope work I've been practicing," said Bernard fingering the nylon rope slung over his right shoulder.

Mike looked up at the digital display and saw that it was 9 am. "We better get moving. We have to check in and find out what track we're leaving on. There's a McDonalds down in the station. We'll grab a quick breakfast before the train pulls out."

The four young people gathered their gear and baggage and with a rising sense of excitement descended the escalator toward the huge terminal below. Walking past stores filled with interesting items, Mike wished that he had arrived a little earlier and explored this little city below street level. Bernard asked the ticket agent for information on the Kentucky-bound train and was directed to Track 12 — destination Louisville, Kentucky with a fifteen-minute stopover in Washington, D.C.

They boarded the *Silver Chief* and stored their gear on overhead racks. Each took a window seat, not wanting to miss anything. Except for Tran, none of the four had ever been outside New York State. The train filled with smiling travelers, mostly vacationers except for a few poker-faced businessmen. After a short wait the train slowly pulled out of the huge terminal and lumbered quietly around sharp curves as it gradually picked up speed. Fifteen minutes later it broke free of the dark tunnels into the bright sunlit metropolis of Newark, New Jersey.

Factories and smokestacks gave way to ghetto housing and rooftops, switching stations and large industrial complexes. In a half-hour's time they were traveling 100 miles an hour over waterways and through suburban countryside. This was an America Mike had never seen before and he liked what he saw; large spacious fields, houses with backyards and spacious school grounds. He looked around at his friends. Lydia had gotten a game of *Trivial Pursuit* started with Tran and Bernard. Mike joined them.

"Lovebirds are indigenous to what country?" asked Lydia.

"New York City," Bernard piped up.

"No. Africa, silly." She looked over at Mike and he noticed her face blush ever so slightly.

He felt attracted to her vulnerability and playfully leaned his head on her shoulders and said: **"I** think Bernard is right. Lovebirds are from New York City."

They both blushed simultaneously and the group broke out in laughter as the train passed through a tunnel momentarily dousing the overhead lights.

"Stop! Don't! How dare you!" Bernard squealed mimicking Lydia's voice as the lights came on. Tran was laughing so much he slid off his seat. When the lights came on and Mike saw him on the floor he roared with laughter. Heads turned to see the source of all the hilarity. Tran regained his seat and tried to maintain his composure.

"Let's behave," Mike said suppressing a grin. Then he couldn't restrain himself and burst out laughing. The conductor entered the car to confirm ticket reservations. Mike got up and made his way toward the snack car stopping first to have the conductor confirm his reservation.

"I'll get Cokes for you guys," he yelled back to his friends as he made his way through the car smiling at passengers and trying to sort out his feelings about Lydia. Leaning on her shoulder he had smelled the freshness of her hair and a trace of perfume. When the lights went out she had said "Michael" softly and with a tinge of surprise.

THE STUYVESANT CONNECTION

He had never thought of her in a romantic way before. A new element had entered into their relationship. Something entirely different was stirring inside of him and he liked it. Entering the lounge car, a porter was attending to several people at a mini-bar. Others were seated at tables playing cards and sipping Cokes. A group of teen-agers was tossing a girl's compact back and forth out of reach of her grasping hands.

A blond, crew-cut teenager rose from his seat, intercepted the tossed compact and said: "Karen, you won't be needing this. Nobody's going to be seeing you in a cave."

"Give it back, Butch!" said the auburn-haired girl as she pulled his hand from his pocket and retrieved her compact.

"You guys going to Mammoth in Kentucky?" asked Mike getting Butch's attention.

"Yea, how'd you know?" asked Butch with surprise.

"I'm from Stuyvesant High School in New York City," said Mike extending his hand.

"We're from Fort Lee High in New Jersey," said Butch shaking the proffered hand. Mike nodded to the others who smiled and nodded back.

"You guys ever go cave exploring before? This will be our first time. My friends are in the 3rd car," volunteered Mike.

"Yea, since we heard we won the Science Essay we've been exploring old mine shafts in Quarryville, New Jersey and a few small caves near there. When we get to Mammoth we want to explore a few side shafts during the wild caving tour." Butch said as he eyed his friends in some kind of secret communication.

"I think those cave passages are assigned and we'll be having experienced guides along. Right, Butch?" asked Mike surprised at their boldness in exploring side shafts without a guide.

"Yea, supposedly," said Butch resignedly, as he pushed both hands deeply into his denim pockets. "But we would like to make our own connections. You see, I've been to Mammoth before with my dad. He's an experienced caver but wasn't able to come along. I know the area pretty good."

"Uh, hmm," said a dark-haired youth, breaking off the conversation.

Butch invited Mike and his friends to join their group in the lounge car after lunch for a game of cards. As Mike left the group, he heard the one called Tony admonish Butch for revealing their plan to do a little side exploring.

After ordering Cokes, Mike precariously made his way back to his friends as the *Silver Chief* rounded a wide curve at 90 miles an hour. Just as he was about to place the Cokes on their lap tables the train went into another curve and he started to fall in the seat opposite theirs. Bernard and Tran lunged toward him and grabbed at his shirt and hauled him in, dripping Cokes and all. Lydia laughed at the Chaplinesque scene. Mike settled down, distributed the Cokes, and recounted his meeting with the group from Fort Lee, including their secretive attempt to do some cave exploring on their own.

"Sounds dangerous to me" said Tran. "Did you know that amateur cave exploration results in hundreds of deaths and injuries each year? The only way to do it safely is to belong to a speleological club and learn with a group."

"A speleological club, what's that?" Bernard stuttered.

"It's a group of people who are interested in the science of exploring caves. They pool all their knowledge and conduct cave exploration under supervised conditions until each caver is a well-trained spelunker."

A spelunker, what's that?" joked Bernard feigning ignorance. "A person whose hobby is exploring caves, silly," chimed in Lydia. "Boy, Bernard you're dumb!"

"Ah, who needs training? All you need is some good clothing, plenty of light, and a ball of string you can let out as you go along. I bought several hundred feet of nylon rope and read up on rock climbing. I've even practiced a few climbers' knots to handle different situations. I'm ready. How about you, Mike?"

THE STUYVESANT CONNECTION

"Well, I agree with Tran. Caving can be a very dangerous activity without proper supervision. In 1974 Mammoth was connected to Flint Ridge making it the longest mapped cave in the world. Attempts have been made to connect Joppa Ridge with Mammoth but so far they have resulted in failure and in some cases the cavers have never been seen again."

"You mean they died?"

"They've never been found and it's presumed that's what happened. It's a particularly nasty system with numerous cave-ins and rock falls reported."

"You'd have to be crazy to attempt a connection in a system like that" Tran said.

"What's the matter, Tran? You chicken!" goaded Bernard.

"No, I just learned from experience how lucky I was to get out of Cambodia when I did. With Pol Pot slaughtering millions of Cambodians and the North Vietnamese decimating our country, I made it through some pretty harrowing experiences. Life, especially in this country, is so precious that I don't ever want to tempt fate and risk it foolishly."

"Bernard, I hope you and Michael aren't planning any cave explorations on your own, are you?" asked Lydia.

Michael's eyes widened at the question. He looked at Bernard and saw an animated desire for adventure in his eyes. Michael picked up a card from the *Trivia* board and laughed with surprise at the question.

"What is the name of the young slave who mapped and explored the Mammoth Cave System and became its' most famous guide?"

"Stephen Bishop!" said Bernard with evident pride. Mike had an intuitive feeling that minute that this was going to be more than an ordinary tour.

THE STUYVESANT CONNECTION

MAMMOTH CAVE
NATIONAL PARK
A World Heritage Site
and International Biosphere Reserve

CHAPTER VI

The train whistled through the Kentucky countryside. Michael felt drawn into the landscape by the speeding train. Here and there horses dotted the carpeted green fields. Some sought protection against the mid-day sun under the forested canopy of clusters of oak trees scattered among the rolling fields.

Michael knew that beneath this tranquil scene was another world of limestone deposited hundreds of millions of years ago. Before the continent of North America rose out of the sea, coral, sponges, clams, snails and other shellfish abounded. Over eons of time the accumulated debris of calcium carbonate from their shells formed into limestone. Since the limestone beds laid down by the sea creatures were softer than the rock formations, underground brooks and streams gently carved great caves and winding passages out of the solid limestone.

As the train entered the city of Louisville, Tran, Lydia, and Bernard returned to their seats and prepared to disembark from the train.

"Hey, Bernie, I had fun playing *Rummy 500* against Butch and his friends. You know Butch knows a lot about Mammoth. He's been here before with his father. Too bad they're in another group. We could have had some fun together. Well, guess we'll run into them during the tour" Mike said as he pulled in his seat to let Bernie get near the window.

The foursome gathered up their books, games, and magazines and prepared to disembark from the train. The train slowly glided into the busy metro station of Louisville, Kentucky. The conductor announced a 15 minute stopover for people heading further south. Mike and his group headed for a small kiosk as directed in the itinerary. There they were met by a smiling, blue-eyed young man who introduced himself as Todd Green, their guide and companion during their stay at Mammoth. He directed them to a blue van for the 85 mile drive to Mammoth National Park.

"You all must be a bit tired of sleeping on those hard coach seats last night. I think you'll enjoy the accommodations we have for you at the lodge" said Todd.

"Yea, the first ten hours were great, you know, looking at the scenery and all. Last night though, it sure was difficult getting some sleep. It seemed we were stopping every half hour, loading and unloading people," volunteered Michael.

"How long you been working at Mammoth, Todd? asked Lydia.

"This is my third year. I attend the University of Louisville where I'm majoring in geology. Working at Mammoth during semester breaks and during the summer pays for part of my tuition. I'm also a member of the Cave Research Foundation and I get updated information on any new passages discovered."

"That sounds interesting" Mike said.

"It is. My friends and I explore passages not open to the public. Last summer we connected with the Flint Ridge System via passages discovered in 1974. It took us 20 hours of arduous spelunking but we finally made it."

"We were lucky we had a map. Makes you appreciate what those original explorers accomplished. It was hell for us, imagine what they must have went through!" said Todd.

"Is Mammoth the largest cave system in the world?" asked Tran.

"It has over 300 miles of mapped passages. Caves, with rooms the size of many football fields have been discovered in Indonesia but Mammoth is the longest known mapped cave system that exists. If a long-sought connection is made to Joppa Ridge, then I don't see how it could ever be surpassed" said Todd.

"During your period of wild caving I'll accompany you and we'll explore sections by kerosene lamp. You'll get a kick out of that. Just keep in mind the need for safety. Caving can be dangerous. Every year hundreds of lives are lost through inexperience and risk-taking on the part of neophyte explorers" said Todd.

Mike saw him catch a glance of each one of them as if he were pondering who was the reckless one in this group. Lydia gave Mike an "I told you so" expression which Michael avoided. Michael took in the beautiful scenery. They were passing through blue-grass country. Spirited horses galloped through a sea of fenced in deep green fields. Barns and stables dotted the countryside.

Todd told the group about the history and development of the Mammoth National Park System and about the personalities who made the area famous. It was discovered by a settler who tracked a wounded bear down its historic entrance. During the War of 1812 and the Civil War it was used as a saltpeter mine. Even Jesse James had visited Mammoth country, holding up a stagecoach during its ten-mile run to Cave City.

Among its earliest visitors was a pre-historic Indian who made his way by the light of reed torches in the fourth century B.C. He ventured two miles into the darkness to mine gypsum for ceremonial paint. He was killed by a shifting boulder and his body became mummified in the cave atmosphere. He was found in 1935 by two guides. The first person to make extended tours of the cave system and to map many of its most famous passages was a young slave named Stephen Bishop. He started exploring the cave in 1838 and became its most famous guide. Todd asked the group about their winning essays and became engrossed in their explanations.

The van rode alongside a body of water that appeared out of the park's leafy forest. "That's the Green River, folks," said Todd. "Rainwater seeps into the limestone and creates ideal cave-making conditions. It carves underground passages as it flows into the Green River. This area has a 500-foot-thick layer of limestone. The shafts and passages are the routes created by the water as it converges into underground rivers that flow into the Green River."

The van climbed a steep grade where it leveled off and glided between the huge portals that marked the entrance of the Mammoth

Lodge. The young people gathered their gear and followed Todd through the lobby. Teenagers gathered in groups just off the lobby where there was comfortable seating and where the soft melodic fingering of a piano could be heard. The lodge was warm and cozy. Todd checked with the desk and soon had keys to their rooms. The boys would room together while Lydia would be sharing a room with two other girls. They went to their rooms to freshen up and agreed to meet at noon for lunch.

In the lodge cafeteria hundreds of teenagers conversed over the clamorous din of dishes, silverware and sliding chairs. The food was good and served smorgasbord style. Mike and Bernard went for the steak and fries while Lydia and Tran chose the shrimp fried rice and boiled vegetables. Groups from other schools were excitedly describing the wonders of their subterranean tours. After lunch, they meandered into the piano room where a talented pianist was playing "The Sting," Scott Joplin's ragtime piano piece. Mike and Bernard were drawn to the room by the catchy tune and got into a conversation with the pianist, a sixteen-year-old boy from Philadelphia.

After a while Mike left the room and joined Tran and Lydia as they gazed at the Mammoth countryside through a large picture window. Begonias and other flowers hung in profusion from wicker baskets and added a pleasant scent to the surroundings. To the right of the window was a library and sitting room. Several teenagers were lazily ensconced in cozy velvet armchairs that faced a large stone fireplace. They were browsing through past issues of *National Geographic* taken from the bookshelves that lined the wall of the library.

Mike wandered over to a large map which geographically outlined the twisting passages and major discoveries made at Mammoth. Pictures of the more famous personalities and their exploits lined the wall. A small room just off the library was dedicated to the Cave Research Foundation, the source of modern day discoveries and the scientific arm of Mammoth National Park.

THE STUYVESANT CONNECTION

Mike was fascinated by the description of the more recently discovered passages and the arduous exploration that had uncovered them. Some journeys into the cave system were thirty to forty hours in duration. The connection that united Mammoth to the Flint Ridge System took decades and was made up of one small discovery added to another.

Mike left the room and joined Tran and Lydia and a group of teenagers who were gathered around Bernard who was improvising at the piano. At one point the boy from Philadelphia interspersed segments of the "The Sting" into Bernard's improvisation and a lively tune drew applause from those gathered around the piano. After Bernard had finished, Mike asked his friends if they wanted to accompany him to a spot he had seen on the map where several large sinkholes existed.

Mike's friends joined him as they walked from the lodge to a natural corridor of oak trees which extended for a half mile before opening up into the deep green hills of the Mammoth countryside. Dappled sunlight broke through the trees at intervals. Large green fields dipped and rose in undulating mounds on both sides of the corridor. After a short walk, they came upon a sign directing them to "The Blowing Hole." A chasm fifteen-feet wide and twenty-five-feet long opened up before them. Cool moist air emanated from it.

"This area is full of sinkholes. Rainwater enters into these sinkholes which in turn creates passages that eventually flow into the Green River. It is a living cave system. That means it is still growing in size" said Mike to his friends as he threw a small stone into the gaping hole.

"Kind of creepy, isn't it? Finding a gaping hole in the middle of nowhere. Good thing they have a small fence around it," said Tran.

They each took turns firing stones into the hole: Bernard heaved a small boulder into the chasm.

"Sounds like a hundred-foot-drop," said Mike as he listened for a ricochet.

"Yea, about that," said Bernard.

THE STUYVESANT CONNECTION

They threw a few more stones then they turned away from "The Blowing Hole" and made their way back to the lodge. They were all kind of quiet.

THE STUYVESANT CONNECTION

CHAPTER VII

Mike was speaking to Lydia as other students meandered in groups under a huge old Kentucky oak tree situated just outside the lodge. Bernard and Tran joined them on a bench that girdled the old oak tree. Todd came bounding down the steps of the lodge, smiling at the students who were eager to make the half mile walk to the Historic Entrance of Mammoth. Todd led the group up a hilly trail that began behind the lodge. Todd recounted the discovery of the Historic Entrance. Mike imagined himself the farmer coming upon the entrance after searching for the wounded bear.

At the entrance a thin waterfall splattered thirty feet into the rocky, leaf-strewn floor. The cave entrance looked dark and ominous to Mike. The students filed slowly behind Todd along a rocky hallway that was bathed in fluorescent light. Mike zippered his nylon windbreaker in response to the constant fifty-four-degree temperature of the cave. It smelled like a dank cellar. The students gasped as they came into an enormous room. From the map he had studied at the lodge, Mike knew that they were in the Rotunda. The room was about 150 feet long and just as wide. The ceiling was forty feet above them. The students listened intently as Todd explained that slaves had mined saltpeter from the orange soil beneath their feet. The saltpeter was used in making gunpowder during the War of 1812.

"Listen," said Mike to his friends. The sound of slaves laboring and coaxing oxen along came from a hidden recorder. The recording realistically created in Mike's imagination a picture of men laboring in the relentless darkness aided only by kerosene torches. The low, moaning sound of oxen pulling carts loaded with barrels of saltpeter made Mike look at the orange soil beneath his feet for wagon tracks.

The students continued along a wide passageway called Broadway. At one point Mike saw Todd reach toward a recess in the

45

wall. The fluorescent lights sputtered out. Lydia grabbed Mike's arm. There were sounds of utter fright and alarm. The group of students froze in the sudden blackness. Lydia clung to Michael. Bernard gave out a yell. Mike could feel his heart beating.

Todd's voice broke through with reassurance. "This is the traditional lights out ceremony. I'm sorry I startled you but I wanted you to get the full impact of the darkness early cave explorers met with. As you can see, it makes an impact. Now I want to show you how early cave explorers were able to light up large areas," a butane lighter broke the eerie darkness and then a sudden flash enveloped them as Todd lit kerosene rags weighted with rocks and tossed them out into the darkness. They lit up various corners of a wide area before sputtering out.

"We even have our own torches along to recreate the same conditions early explorers experienced." He passed out kerosene lanterns to the students. The young people grinned in the orange-yellow glow of the kerosene lamps. Mike followed Todd as he led them down a narrow rocky path to Fat Man's Misery, a hundred feet of narrow, twisting passage less than six-feet-high. Mike could move his arms but his legs scraped the side of the passage as he nudged forward. An ancient stream had sculpted Fat Man's Misery.

After passing through Fat Man's Misery they came to a towering chamber called Mammoth Dome. The students began the long ascent up a 138-step metal staircase. Mike marveled at the beautiful coloration of the formations along the wall. Impurities had seeped into the calcite turning stalagmites, columns, flowstone, and stalactites into a beautiful array of colors. Mike felt transported to another world, so colorful was all the imagery. Reaching the top of the dome, they exited a passageway that took them to the Rotunda again.

"The tour you just completed is the Historic Tour. I hope you liked it. Tomorrow we are going to take the Echo River Tour. It's an hour longer and filled with interesting passages. We'll be heading back to the lodge for lunch. The rest of the afternoon belongs to you. Those of you who want a change of pace can avail yourself of the many activities within walking distance of the lodge, like horseback riding, swimming, archery, and other activities listed on the directory back at the lodge. We meet again as a group at 9:30 am in the library. Until then, enjoy yourself" said Todd.

Later that evening after a day of horseback riding at the Ponderosa, a stable located about a mile from the lodge, Michael and his friends sat on chaise lounges near the swimming pool. Vapors from a whirlpool clouded the glass enclosure that encircled the pool. Mike got up from his lounge chair and toweled a section of glass in order to see the sun setting over the Kentucky countryside.

"I really felt like a cowboy today. My horse was so responsive, I could have taken him anywhere" said Mike throwing the towel back on the chaise lounge. "How was yours, Lydia?" he asked.

"Mine was a bit frisky but calmed down once the barn was out of sight. In the open field, I felt like I was on a racehorse and held on for dear life. Now I know how a jockey feels," Lydia said draping a towel about her full figure as she sat back.

"How'd you like the tour this morning, Mike? asked Bernard, rubbing his eyes. "Too much chlorine in the pool!"

"I thought it was an electrical failure when the lights went out. The· blackness was unbelievable. The rest of the tour using the kerosene lamps was neat. I'm looking forward to the river tour tomorrow," said Mike watching the sun cast a red glow over the distant hillside.

"I was thinking of how I could find my way out once the lights went out. I knew we were several hundred feet from the Historic Entrance and I was trying to remember the major trail obstacles. I think I could have found my way back if there had been a real emergency" said Tran rising from his lounge chair and executing a perfect racing dive that took him halfway across the pool.

At 9:30 am the next morning Todd led the group through the Historic Entrance, past the Rotunda, down Broadway to a large slanting pile of rubble. They ascended a small path that led to an opening in the pile of rubble. The sound of rushing water became distinct as they approached a wide stream Todd called the River Styx. Water poured from an opening high atop River Hall and settled in a narrow underground river. Todd directed the group into a flat-bottomed boat that seated twelve people. He motioned to Mike to man a large pole to push the boat away from the make-shift dock. The boat gently glided forward into the widening stream of water.

Mike marveled at the· beauty of the subterranean world they were gliding through. Stalagmites rose from the water as stalactites bit into the River Styx. Recessed lighting played on the multicolored formations. Mike felt as if he were navigating a lunar lake somewhere in space. The other young passengers aboard the boat seemed to be transfixed at the beauty of nature that was unfolding before them. The River Styx widened into a large body of water called Lake Lethe. At various points vents fed water to the lake. On its way down the water had polished and worn away the limestone into a perfect waterslide

Mike imaginded himself sliding down the fluted vents and swimming to one of the large stalagmites that rose from the center of the lake. Todd and Mike pushed on until they came to Echo River. Looking down, Mike could see streaks of silver darting away every time he immersed the pole into the water. He knew that it was probably a troglobite, a blindfish that never ventured from the cave environment. At one point Todd showed them a black-eyed cave salamander that he scooped up from a nearby rock.

Pushing on, Todd pointed out a large opening to the right where the river forked. It was an underground stream that ran 5,000 feet before it fed into the Green River. Poling further on the group came to a huge lake called Cascade Hall. It had a natural limestone dock. Todd pointed to a dark opening in the distance. It was there that a group of spelunkers emerged from a watery passageway and made the historic connection from Flint Ridge to Mammoth.

THE STUYVESANT CONNECTION

The group sat around the dock and ate lunch. They wanted to go swimming in the crystal-clear water of Cascade Hall but park regulations forbade it. Todd informed them that they had reached the end of their Echo River tour. Bernard volunteered to replace Mike at the stern and pole the group back to the River Styx.

Back at the lodge Todd was summoned to a hushed conversation with a park official. A look of concern and seriousness changed his usually smiling demeanor as he gathered the group around him.

"We have a problem here. It looks like we might have to cancel tomorrow's tour. Five students from Fort Lee, New Jersey are missing and we suspect the worst. There is a possibility they are trapped or lost in one of the caves in the surrounding area. All National Park personnel are being organized to conduct a search."

"Hey Mike, weren't Butch and Tony from Fort Lee?" asked Bernard.

"They were, and I remember they kind of hinted they were experienced cavers and wanted to explore some virgin caves in the area. Butch seemed to know the area. His father is an amateur spelunker and had taken him caving here before. They had been looking for some kind of connection to Mammoth at the time. I wish I could remember the area he mentioned."

"In any case, unless they are found by tonight, we'll have to cancel the tour for tomorrow. Consider it a free day. You can go horseback riding or even visit one of the public tours to nearby caves. And, Mike, if you can recall the area where these kids might have gone, let me know," said Todd.

"Why can't we go along and help you look for them?" asked Mike. "We've gotten some experience."

"We can't take the chance of searching with inexperienced cavers. If these kids took some of the lesser known passages, they've exposed themselves to all kinds of dangers, rockfalls, spring flooding, and probably inadequate lighting to name a few. Besides you would probably slow us down. Most of the staff here are familiar with many of the lesser known passages. Well, we've got work to do" said Todd as he walked back to the waiting official.

The Stuyvesant group went to the library area and looked out the large picture window that framed the Kentucky countryside.

"Come on, you guys. Let's look at the map in the other room. Maybe it'll jog my memory. Butch said something about making a connection to Mammoth from some ridge or something like that," said Mike.

Consulting the map Mike pointed to the historic connection made in 1972 when the Flint Ridge System was connected to Mammoth. He had read about the obsession to unite the two systems making Mammoth the largest cave system in the world.

"Could that be it? Were they trying to retrace the connection? It's off limits to tourist now." Running his finger along the Mammoth-Flint Ridge map, he called out the principal cave entrances that Butch and his group might have entered. "Onyx Cave, Crystal Cave, Salt Cave, Colossal Cave, Sand Cave — that's the cave Floyd Collins got stuck in and where he died. Frozen Niagra, The Carmichael Entrance, Violet City or the Historic Entrance. Take your pick! Let's see, here's the Flint Ridge connection — if you start at Mammoth it begins in Cascade Hall where Echo River runs through. It leads to Hanson's Lost River under Flint Ridge to the Tight Spot, then to Tight Tube, up the Bretz River to the Austin Entrance. What do you think? Were they retracing the connection made in 1972?"

Tran nodded assent. Lydia and Bernard thought it made sense.

"Or," Mike said, looking squarely at them. "Could they have been trying to make a new connection? If you look at the map, you could see that Houchin's Valley connected Mammoth to Flint Ridge. The only other major valley that remains unconnected is the Doyel Valley. That would unite Joppa Ridge to Mammoth. It's never been connected. Explorers believe that someday it will be connected. I think that's what they tried to do. Butch mentioned his father was a veteran cave explorer. I'm willing to bet that they're in the Joppa Ridge System. Probably lost because it's not well-surveyed and is considered dangerous due to numerous breakdowns. Let's find Todd. Maybe he'll let us tag along."

They met Todd, and Mike outlined all he had heard about making a connection. Todd was sure they were trying to retrace the epic connection that led Mammoth to Flint Ridge since it was the only mapped connection available. He downplayed Mike's theory about the Joppa Ridge connection. What would school kids know about the treacherous Joppa Ridge System? Numerous attempts by experienced cavers had all met with frustration and an occasional injury due to the unstable nature of the cave resulting in breakdown. Todd thanked Mike and after much cajoling and prodding agreed to consult his superior to see if the group could tag along at least for the first half-day of the rescue attempt. He would try to get it credited toward their wild caving time.

Receiving permission to take the Stuyvesant group along with him for no longer than four hours, Todd gave them a list of equipment they would need and could draw from the Rescue Station. They were to meet at the Historic Entrance in two hours to begin the search.

Leaving the meeting with Todd, Mike felt that Todd was probably right. Why would a group of inexperienced cavers try to make a connection from Joppa Ridge? They had probably stayed behind last night after their main tour and attempted to retrace the connection to Flint Ridge from Mammoth. It was the only thing that made sense. An image of Butch's facial expression the last time he saw him fleetingly came to mind. Butch had his own agenda before he even got here, thought Michael.

CHAPTER VIII

At the main Rescue Station the Stuyvesant group received their shoulder packs. In each pack was a First Aid kit, knee crawlers, canned food, a can opener, a water bottle, heat tabs, nylon rope, three lighting sources, a compass and carbide bottles for their lamps. Todd showed them how the carbide lamps worked. He also showed Tran how to use a survey chain in case they found a new passage and had to map it. Todd smiled when he saw each one wearing a New York Mets batting helmet.

Todd led them into the Historic Entrance down the rubble strewn Houchins Narrows to the Rotunda. They passed the saltpeter works to Broadway and got through Fat Man's Misery. They stopped to relieve themselves in the restroom at Great Relief Hall. From there they continued on to the River Styx where they boarded the flat-bottom boat. Bernard manned the large pole at the stern of the boat and gently glided forward into the widening stream. After a while they entered Lake Lethe and marveled at the beauty of the subterranean lake. The sound of rushing water pouring from vents into the lake heightened the sense of their underground rescue.

What a story to tell when we get back, thought Mike, almost glad that Butch had gotten into such a mess. Wouldn't it be cool if we can find Butch and his classmates? Mike could see the headlines in the school newspaper, "Stuyvesant High students rescue lost teens in daring cave rescue."

They came to a fork where the waterway connected to the Green River. Staying left, they entered Cascade Hall. A roaring sound of water pouring from limestone smooth water chutes into Cascade Hall made Mike think that Butch had probably tried the waterslide and had done some swimming before entering the Cascade connection.

THE STUYVESANT CONNECTION

They anchored the boat at the natural limestone dock and sat down for a snack of apples and peanut butter and jelly sandwiches they had made in the lodge dining room before meeting with Todd.

"Well gang, here's your chance to do four hours of wild caving. We're going to be entering an underwater passage, well up into your neck in places. Anyone wanting to stay behind, here is your chance; you can wait at the dock. We'll be returning in four hours," said Todd

Mike looked at Lydia. She looked concerned but said nothing. Todd passed out lightweight, waterproof clothing that slipped easily over their outerwear and buttoned at the neck. The group re-entered the flat-bottom boat and headed for the miniscule opening into Cascade Hall on the far-right wall at water level. Mike felt a rising sense of exhilaration as they neared their goal. Wild caving was about to begin. Very few people had been beyond this point.

The boat bit into the sandbank at the far wall. The group disembarked and followed Todd over a stretch of sand to a pool of water. A small opening could be seen above the water level at the far end of the pool of water. Todd led the group down the muddy embankment searching for footprints and any evidence that someone had been there recently. Mike could see a note of puzzlement on his face. Mike followed closely behind as Todd entered the water up to his waist. Mike groaned as the coldness of the water penetrated through the plastic liner. Ducking under an eighteen-inch opening they held their shoulder sacks over their heads.

"Lucky for us the spring flooding has subsided. There are times when this slot is completely flooded" said Todd.

"What would happen if we had heavy rains right now?" asked Mike.

"I guess we would have to find another way outta here," said Todd nonchalantly.

The going got a bit easier once they slogged through the first thirty feet. Mike marveled at the multicolored jagged beauty of the ceiling. At one point the passage split, one branch occupied by a stream, the other a cut-around. The group followed the cut-around whenever it could. Todd informed the group they were now passing under Ganter Avenue and were heading northeast toward Flint Ridge.

The passage seemed endless. Mike could feel his heart pounding. Pete Hanson and Leo Hunt had explored this passage in 1938, long before the final connection was made. Mike had read about it in *The Longest Cave* last night. He knew they had turned back at some point but not before leaving their initials scratched in the muddy walls. Those same initials had given euphoria to the group that came upon them after twenty hours searching for a connection. Once they saw the initials they knew it was only a matter of time before they connected with Mammoth Cave. Pete and Leo believed that this had been a false lead and never came back to it again.

As the group pushed forward the passage got smaller.

"I'm thirsty, can we stop for water?" asked Lydia.

They stopped for a water break.

"This passage is getting kind of narrow, isn't it Todd?" said Lydia as she rubbed her aching knees. "Do these passages ever cave in?" she asked as she pried a loose rock near her foot.

"Rarely, unless you disturb the supporting strata," said Todd.

Lydia quickly dropped the rock as if it were hot.

"Do you want to turn back Lydia?" asked Todd

She looked around at her friends and declined. Todd placed her behind himself and had Mike bring up the rear in the next crawlway they entered.

Entering the crawlway, they walked on all fours. Bernard began to joke about being tired of seeing rear-ends instead of faces. Finally, they entered a muddy room. In the corner was another crawlway where water trickled out. Todd searched the area meticulously, looking for tracks in the mud.

THE STUYVESANT CONNECTION

"There's no evidence this passage has been traveled recently," said Todd as he rested his back against a roughhewn wall in an act of resignation. He looked at his wristwatch and said: "We are going to turn back. I gave you an extra hour because you're a good group. You got a taste of wild caving — how did you like it?"

"It was neat" Mike said.

"I'm ready for some more," said Bernie.

"Interesting geological formations," added Tran.

"I'm ready to soak my tired body in a nice hot tub. It made me appreciate the comforts we take for granted at home," said Lydia, adjusting her shoulder sack for the crawl back home.

"Well, let's go. We don't want the Park Supervisor sending out a search party after us. We'll make faster time going back. The Rescue Station will be closed, so you can check your equipment in tomorrow. Maybe when we get back, they'll have found Butch and his friends so we can continue our tour. If not, consider tomorrow a free day and enjoy the activities at the lodge. Time will be of the essence if they haven't found those kids. We'll have to locate them by tomorrow or else we'll be in for big trouble," said Todd as he ducked into the crawlway for the trek back to the boat.

Returning to the lodge at 6 pm, Todd was summoned to the Park Supervisor's office. Mike felt that an atmosphere of anxiety and emergency permeated the lodge. Rescue vehicles and several ambulances from surrounding communities were parked about the lot. Butch and his group had not been found and an all-out search and rescue was into effect. Teens gathered about the lobby in small groups and several were being interviewed by reporters on their response to the loss of their friends. A few had known Butch and described him as bright but reckless and impulsive. Others appeared unconcerned and made plans to use the pool or sign up for horseback riding in the morning.

The Stuyvesant young people went to their rooms to shower and agreed to meet in the dining room for dinner at 6:45 pm. Cleaned and refreshed and only a bit sore from crawling, they took a table near a trio of musicians playing the opening bars to "New York, New York." They were served soup and salad and a main course of venison covered with chestnut sauce, brown rice, and mixed vegetables. For dessert, they all had a sumptuous serving of Black Forest chocolate cake, washed down by cold milk served in long stem glasses.

"Man, that was good" said Bernard wiping his mouth with a burgundy-colored napkin. "I never knew deer meat tasted so good. I gotta learn to hunt."

Behind the musicians' platform a large bay window offered a panoramic view of the Kentucky countryside. Mike watch as the setting sun highlighted the rolling green fields where horses grazed. In the distance a thick green forest reached high into the hills. Somewhere beneath them five teenagers were lost and rescuers, swarming like ants in a maze, were trying to make contact. Mike's eyes followed the hill toward a rocky area about two miles away.

"Joppa Ridge" whispered Mike occupied in thought.

"What did you say?" asked Bernie.

"Joppa Ridge!" said Mike defiantly. "They are in the Joppa Ridge System trying to make a connection to Mammoth. I know it. Butch and his friends spoke of making a connection, not retracing an old one. I know they are in there!"

"Are you crazy, Michael. Professional cavers haven't been able to make a connection. Don't get any hair-brained ideas. Five hours of wild caving and you think you know the system. We're here for a vacation, not to get lost!" said Lydia.

Mike noticed that her eyes widened whenever she got really angry. "I don't know, Lydia, wouldn't it be fun to try and find Butch and his friends? I think they're all searching in the wrong place," said Michael looking around for allies.

"You are crazy, Michael. Who do you think you are, a great white explorer? Well this is one minority you can count out. You've got some nerve trying to con us into your hair-brained scheme. You could endanger all of us. I can just see it now: "Four Stuyvesant

THE STUYVESANT CONNECTION

High School Students Lost Attempting Rescue." Todd warned us and we got to think of our school — we represent it," said Lydia.

Mike noticed her eyes widen and her face grew red with anger as she continued.

"You're spoiling a beautiful evening by talking about a rescue," added Lydia.

Mike looked around. Tran just listened and looked down when Mike looked toward him.

Bernie shifted restlessly then squared his shoulders. "I think we should try it. I worked on rope and climbing techniques back home thinking they'd come in handy. I'd like to try it. I'm not saying we should make an all-out effort."

"That's what I mean, Bernie," said Mike. "We'll set a time limit, say seven hours; then we'll turn back. If we find any evidence of their whereabouts we'll report it to Todd."

Tran looked up and said: "My dad's a geologist for Texaco Oil. I know a lot about cave geology from him. If you set a time limit I'll go along. I'll do some survey maps so we don't get lost. Todd showed me how they're done."

"Tran, I'm with you. Surveying is the best way to do it. If we find them or any evidence of their whereabouts we'll have maps to show the way. They'd also help in any class report we would do on this emergency. And you know... no one has to know we're gone. We'll sign up for horseback riding tonight on tomorrow's activity sheet. No one will look for us tomorrow and we'll be home for dinner. I wouldn't miss dinner for anything," said Mike taking a huge bite of his chocolate cake.

Lydia looked at Tran as if she'd been betrayed. "I think you all are going nuts. "Stuyvesant High School youths lost in a labyrinth" is a more likely report the class will receive. I'm not going with you guys" she said nervously tapping her spoon on the tablecloth.

Mike sensed that her resolve was weakening and he wanted her along. "Lydia, stay on the surface. If we pass our time limit, then seek help from the staff."

THE STUYVESANT CONNECTION

Mike could see that any warmth she might have felt for him was fast turning to cold contempt because of what she perceived as his recklessness. He felt that it was passive to stand by when he knew in his heart that Butch was in the Joppa Ridge System.

"You know, Michael, caving is a dangerous activity especially to the inexperienced. Rockfalls, drowning, bad air, falls and entrapment are just a few of the things that could happen. Could you live with that? One of your friends injured, possibly killed? Could you live with that?"

"Ah, Lydia, you're being too gloomy. We could use you along for First Aid. Stay with us to the point of known exploration, then get ·help if we need it or pass our time limit. But I don't intend to get lost," said Mike with an air of bravado.

The group became silent after a while. Mike looked around as his friends pondered a goal that hadn't existed before something happened in the normal course of events. Things were topsy-turvy and adjustments had to be made. Mike was certain that no one was going to try the Joppa Ridge connection. Something had to be done soon; an effort had to be made, a chance had to be taken. Mike looked at Lydia and understood her anger at his seeming recklessness. A challenge had been thrust upon her. Not to be part of it would mean exclusion from their shared journey. He was relieved when she looked around at her friends and said: "O.K. I'll go."

After dinner, the group went back to the room containing the map of the entire known cave system. After studying the Joppa Ridge System, Mike noticed they could save hours off their trek if they entered Joppa Ridge from a sinkhole several miles from the lodge. He surmised that Butch and his crew had ventured beyond that point and were to be found much deeper in the cave. In order to save time and get around Lydia's time constraint, they would enter Joppa Ridge from the sinkhole.

Mike looked up the meaning of an asterisk near the sinkhole entrance. A broad smile crossed his face as he told Bernard the meaning. "The asterisk states that this entrance is closed to the general public because of precipitous climbing conditions requiring the use of ropes and expert climbing techniques.

"I'm looking forward to this," said Bernard.

Lydia looked at Bernard with a sense of amazement and fear in her face. "Surely you don't believe you're an expert in climbing."

"Not an expert, but pretty good," said Bernard rubbing his chin. "I worked on my climbing technique at Eagle Rock near City College and I read everything on it at the library. I'm looking forward to showing you my rappelling technique and my Prusik belay."

"Prusik belay? What's that?" asked Lydia.

"It's a climbing technique that lets you rest while you ascend a rope" said Bernard.

"First it was Mike, the cave explorer, now it's Bernard, the climbing expert. What's your specialty, Tran?" asked Lydia with a cynical smile.

THE STUYVESANT CONNECTION

CHAPTER IX

Rain pelted the window as the dawn's early light enabled Michael to pack his knapsack. Bernard and Tran slept fitfully until awakened by Michael's busy movements. The thought of wild caving had set Michael's imagination afire and he tossed and turned, unable to sleep for any length of time. Images of crawling through tiny crevices which opened into immense cavernous rooms kept adrenaline coursing through his body. He had even dreamed of climbing down a vertical drop and coming upon an underground river. This fleeting image had given way to the pelting of wind-driven rain against the lodge window.

Mike looked out the window and saw rain-swollen clouds that made him aware of the potential for disaster and the need to prepare for any emergency. Tran and Bernard were now fully awake, packing their own equipment. The greyness of the morning light cast a somber mood about the room that was only broken when Bernard tossed a blue object at Mike and said:

"Mike! Catch!"

Mike fielded the tossed Mets batting helmet and tried it on for size. It fit perfectly. "What's this for? I'm a Yankee fan," he said adjusting the helmet.

"It's for those hardballs that just might come rolling off those cavern walls," said Bernard punching the helmet for impact.

The three boys smiled, the somber mood had been broken, and Mike felt strong and confident in his friend's presence. Leaving the knapsacks in their room, they went down the hall to Lydia's room. She opened the door before they got there. They took her knapsack, deposited it in their room, and went down to breakfast.

The cafeteria had just opened. The smell of coffee brewing, bacon and eggs frying, and the sight of assorted melons and fruit and all kinds of Danishes, set down smorgasbord-style, for the moment distracted Mike from the seriousness of their venture.

THE STUYVESANT CONNECTION

"This rain is like a bad omen," said Lydia, eating a honeydew melon.

"It's not going to be raining where we are going," said Michael offhandedly. "It does, however, increase the chance of flooding and that's not good for Butch and his crew. It makes it imperative that they be found soon." Mike chewed thoughtfully on a toasted bagel.

"I couldn't sleep last night. I kept thinking we'd get lost or trapped in a cave-in" said Lydia sounding depressed. "How about you guys?"

"Like a baby, said Michael smiling, determined to remain optimistic and not give in to his own fears. "Look, we've set a ten... twelve-hour time limit. If we find no sign of them, we return in time for dinner. We're equipped with rescue equipment. Tran will do the surveys. Bernard will be in charge of rope and climbing needs. Lydia, you're in charge of emergency care if needed. We won't take unnecessary chances and safety will be the number one concern. I'll be the group leader, if there are no objections, and I'll determine the passages we take. Oh, and Bernard, think you have something for Lydia."

With that cue, Bernard presented her with a Mets batting helmet. She smiled and they all laughed as Mike reversed the helmet and said, "Gary Carter, guard her."

"From falling rocks and pelting rain," added Tran as he looked out the dining room window.

After a satisfying breakfast, the four friends retrieved their knapsacks. Mike asked the cafeteria manager for four large plastic garbage bags, stating that he and his friends wanted to walk to the riding stables. The manager looked at him in a quizzical manner but acceded to his request. They left the lodge draped in plastic bags and started down the road toward their destination, a cow pasture two miles from the lodge. The rain increased its tempo but the Mets helmets and makeshift raincoats kept the cavers dry and looking forward to the shelter a cave would provide from the driving rain.

THE STUYVESANT CONNECTION

Reaching the pasture, the four spaced apart fifty yards and began to trek forward. The field was lush and mounds of bluegrass softened their footsteps. The first to find a sinkhole was to notify the others by blowing on a whistle. Cows scurried away as the group approached them. Mike saw several cows drinking from a pond. Or was it a pond? He hurried forward and realized that it was the sinkhole they were seeking. The cows were enjoying the upward drafts of cool air the sinkhole provided. He slowed to a walk as he approached the lip of the sinkhole. It was fifty feet across. He blew the whistle and motioned vigorously with his hands, indicating that he had found the entrance to their first wild cave.

"I found it. A big one," Mike said pointing to the abyss.

Tran, Lydia and Bernard stared down the immense, yawning crevice in the earth. On the far side, rivulets of rainwater flowed into the hole. Michael picked up a stone and dropped it into the hole. Several seconds passed before a barely audible ricochet was heard. The four friends looked at each other. Mike pondered whether they should try it or retreat back to the main entrance?

"Let's do it," Mike commanded. "The lodge map said it was seventy-five feet to the bottom. Bernie, it's up to you to get us down there. Safely" he added.

Mike watched as Bernie set down his knapsack and loosened the nylon climbing rope from his shoulders. He looked around for a natural anchor. At first, he picked a jutting rock at the lip of the sinkhole but didn't like the route of descent, it was too steep. Walking around the perimeter for several minutes, he finally chose a split rock outcropping several feet from the sinkhole. He jostled with it several times as a wrestler would to determine that it was soundly embedded. It was situated at the best sloping angle into the sinkhole. Picking up a rock he tied one end of the rope around it. He then wedged it into the split rock as a chock-stop before drawing the rope through the rock. Tugging at it he determined it was safely secured.

THE STUYVESANT CONNECTION

"O.K. folks, you're going to learn how to body rappel down an incline. Who wants to go first? I'll be the last one down because I've got to rig a sling for Lydia. It will be easier for her to manage," Bernard said as he tugged at the rope.

"To get into the body rappel position, face the anchor and stand straddling the rope. This is your holding hand — it will do the main work. Decide what hand you want it to be. In my case, it's the right one. Pull the rope around and in front of you. Lift it over your head and unto the shoulder opposite the holding hand. Are you with me so far?

"The rope will be running between your legs, around your right hip and diagonally across your chest, and over the left shoulder. Reach behind you again with your right hand and grasp the rope hanging off the back of your shoulder. Pull it around your right side again and hold it with your right hand extended downward with your palm up. The holding hand can easily support all your weight. It also controls how fast you descend. The other hand is your balance hand. Place it palm up on the rope in front of you. Don't try to support your weight with this hand. Use it only for balance," Bernard said as he leaned back.

"The toughest part for beginners is getting over the brink." With that said, he sat at the edge with his legs dangling and the rope entwined around his body. Pushing with his balance hand against the side, he spun around into position. "Feed a little rope over your shoulder and lean back until your feet can walk downward," he said as he rappelled a few yards into the yawning chasm.

His three friends yelled and clapped as he lowered himself with seeming ease. Pulling himself up the rope with a strenuous hand over hand effort, he climbed out of the pit. "There is only one problem. With all this rain, the rope is more slippery than usual, so hold tight," he said as he spit into the pit. "Who wants to try it?" he asked.

"I'll go first," volunteered Mike. "What happens if I run out of rope?"

THE STUYVESANT CONNECTION

"You'll have to set another chock or make a decision to come back up. If you do, use this sling as a harness and between the three of us, we'll pull you up. It's not as easy as it looks, Mike, so be careful."

The rain came down in torrents as Mike sat at the edge of the sinkhole entwined in his body rappel. His three friends looked anxious as he rehearsed in his mind the mechanics of body rappelling. The rivulets of water now merged into a small stream on the other side as it disappeared into the void.

Breathing deeply, Mike pushed off the edge with his balance hand. His friends gasped as part of the trailing rope became snagged on the nub of a rock on the precipice, causing Mike's body to be angled awkwardly. With a whip of his holding hand the rope broke free and sailed silently, directly behind him.

"Beautiful, Mike. You're in a good position. To lower yourself, swing the rope around to the side or in back of you," yelled Bernard.

Mike experimented a few minutes with his balance and holding hand to gain the right adjustment. He tried braking by wrapping his right leg around the rope several times. After braking he removed his hands from the rope and displayed them to his friends as a magician would. When both hands were free, palms up; his friends applauded. Gradually he gained more confidence with what he could do. At one point, he leaned back too far and almost lost his balance but gradually felt more comfortable keeping his body straight and leaned back only as much as necessary to keep his feet walking down the rock, looking in the direction he was going.

"You got it! Beautiful position," yelled Bernard in encouragement. "Keep it that way."

Mike began his descent. His friends excitedly shouted encouragement. At fifty feet, an eerie sensation of having been here thousands of years ago, passed through his mind. His friends' shouting became less audible and the sound of water splashing increased in intensity. It wasn't an endless pit after all. It made him feel better.

THE STUYVESANT CONNECTION

At sixty feet, it seems to angle off a bit to the right. He could see the reason why — a large slab of granite protruded through the limestone. It offered a place to rest and examine his surroundings.

Five feet from the ledge, he saw a metallic object hanging over the edge. His heartbeat quickened at the realization that someone had been here recently. Carefully stepping on the ledge, he held the rope and walked toward the metal object.

Turning on his flashlight and kneeling down, he could see that the metallic object had been pounded in the granite at the point of a small crack. Two pieces of rope led off from it. Tugging at the rope and pulling it up he realized it was a rope ladder. As he leaned over the ledge as far as he could, the beam of his flashlight picked up streaming water twenty-five feet below. The other end of the rope ladder disappeared out of sight carried away by the streaming water. He wondered if the heavy rainfall had flooded the passage.

Mike signaled on the rope for Tran to descend. As Tran descended, Mike hollered encouragement and offered a few hints to ease the rappelling down the sinkhole.

"It's a bit hard on the crotch area, eh Tran," said Mike as Tran bounded off the rope to the granite ledge.

"You're not kidding. It's easy to get rope burns if you're not careful," said Tran. "Come here. I want to show you something," said Mike leaning over and pulling up the rope ladder.

"Wow, do you think Butch and his friends used it?" asked Tran.

"I think they intended to return this way but it doesn't make sense not to have prepared a belay at the surface. Why only here? They apparently descended before the rain washout of the passage below. Look here!" Mike said pointing the beam of his light at the swirling water twenty-five feet below.

"That rope ladder disappears into an underground river. I've got to get a better look at what lies below. It may be that the passage is flooded. I'll use the rope ladder if it's safe," Mike added kicking at the top rung as he tested it for strength.

THE STUYVESANT CONNECTION

After determining that it was still in good condition, he began to descend the ladder. Bernard was calling down, informing them that Lydia was about to descend on a sling and would use the rappelling rope as a backup safety line. Tran returned to the rope and yelled encouragement as Lydia descended.

As Mike lowered himself, a damp, musky odor wafted across the sinkhole. Water rolled off the ledge and saturated his clothing. On the other side a small waterfall became a crescendo as it hit the swirling water below drowning out the voices from above.

The ladder began to get slippery from the algae and fungi inhabiting the wet passage. Suddenly he lost his footing. Frantically he tried to regain it. His flashlight broke loose from his slipping grip and rebounded off the wall as it disappeared from sight. Desperation and panic gripped him as he hung suspended, flailing frantically with his feet, trying to get a toehold somewhere.

Mike could hear Tran calling out to him. The rungs had rotted away on the ladder below him. Hand-over-hand, he attempted to raise himself back to the safety of the granite ledge. His body was now thoroughly soaked from the water trickling off the ledge. When he grasped the rung above him so that his foot could find the safety of a lower rung, it snapped. He hit the raging water below feet first and was consumed by a swirling darkness.

Bobbing up and down, he was pulled and tossed by the current into a black void. He grabbed at his spare flashlight that was tucked into his parachute pants. The current pulled him under and he experienced the horrific fear of drowning in the black, cold, underground river. Finally, the dangerous undertow released him and he bobbed up gasping for breath. The dark void gave way to joy as he grasped for the flashlight and snapped the light on. He was in a huge, rain-swollen underground passage.

Casting the beam of his flashlight ahead he could make out a rocky embankment coming up on his right. Mike kicked frantically to level his body and swam diagonally for the embankment. Exhausted and drained he waded into calmer water and fell to his knees on the rocky bank, oblivious to the sharp stones bruising his flesh.

He lay there several minutes trying to comprehend what he had just been through. He cradled the flashlight lovingly, thankful for man's resourcefulness in inventing the light. He felt that now he knew what absolute terror was. It was total darkness, swirling, cold and wet. It terrorized the soul.

He closed his eyes, snapped off his flashlight and rested. It had taken all his strength to swim out of the current. He estimated that he was several hundred yards from his friends and would have to make his way back. Picking himself up, he played the flashlight about his surroundings. The river was about forty feet across widening and narrowing at different points. It was amazing that he hadn't struck any of the huge boulders that protruded from the raging water.

There was a whole new world waiting to be explored. He said a silent prayer for Butch and his friends knowing something of what they must be going through. He hoped that they had sought safety from the rising flood of water.

Climbing over several boulders he rejoiced that the passage offered cutaways and an embankment. Mike began to feel a rising sense of confidence in himself. It had been a harrowing experience, losing one flashlight and regaining another. He was convinced that they had come prepared and were well supplied for at least ten hours or so. This is the right trail, he told himself.

In the distance, he could hear the echoing sound of his friends shouting. Wet, bruised and muddied he scrambled along the rocky embankment and yelled back at his friends: "I'm O.K! It's incredible, but I'm O.K."

THE STUYVESANT CONNECTION

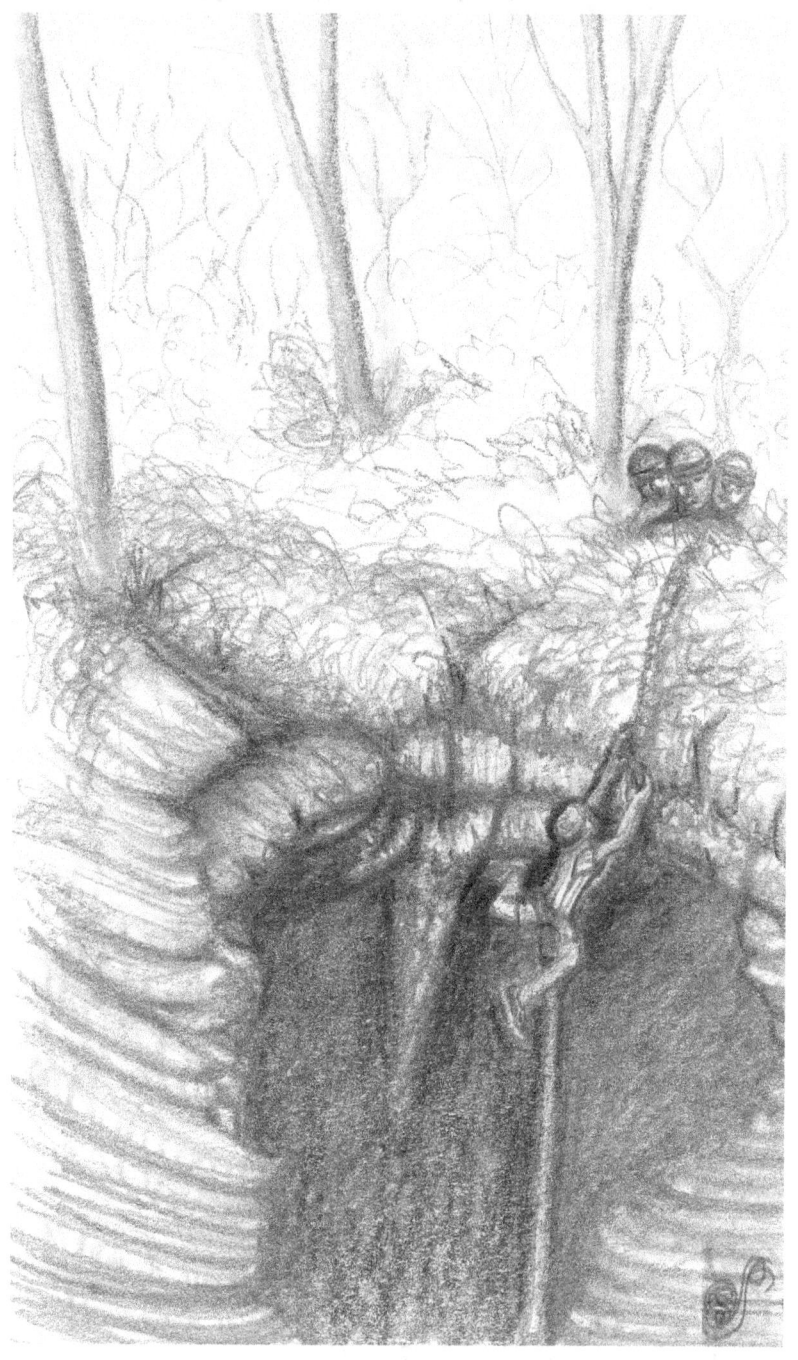

CHAPTER X

Following the beacon of Bernard's light in the distance, Mike made his way over slippery boulders to his friend's side. Bernard had secured a line from an opening in the ceiling of the cavern to a rocky spire rising up from the embankment.

"You O.K, Mike? You had me worried for a while. I thought for sure you had hit one of the boulders in midstream and were unconscious. I tied a rope around my waist. Tran played it out as I swam to the side. It wasn't easy. I'm trying to hook up a pulley to bring Lydia and Tran over here."

"Except for a few bruises, I'm fine," said Mike brushing off the encrusted mud from his face and body. "Bernie, we're in an underground river that goes for miles. Downstream it widens into almost a canyon. It's so beautiful — stalactites and stalagmites, rising fifty feet to the ceiling! There are flat plateaus for camping along the bank and numerous side passages leading to God know where."

"Great, but first we got to get Tran and Lydia down here. Mike, if anyone falls from the pulley, you're going to have to swim and get them. Ready, Lydia!" hollered Bernie.

"Here goooees" cried Lydia moving rapidly toward them on the racing pulley. Mike reached and grabbed her as her feet dragged along the water, slowing her progress.

"I did it! I did it! You did it, Bernie" cried Lydia as she embraced Michael.

"Are you O.K, Michael? We were so worried."

Mike reassured her and then set about helping Bernie bring their knapsacks in. They were loaded into netting by Tran and came skidding along. Tran followed after but not before setting up a reverse line that would enable them to return via the pulley setup to the hole in the cavern wall. Tran was soaked from all the rainwater pouring into the passage.

THE STUYVESANT CONNECTION

Mike told the group what he had seen. "I think we have to stay with the river. Odds are against Butch and his crew opting to explore the numerous passages you'll see along the river bank."

"Any supposed connection would have to be via an underground stream or river. Following a river trail is the only thing that makes sense. That's the only route a rescue team would take," Tran said.

"Hope we don't have to be rescued," added Lydia as she passed around an apple and a candy bar to each of her friends.

"Don't worry Lydia. We have a plan and we'll stick to it. If we don't find them, we'll be back at the lodge before 10 pm" said Mike.

"We'll find them" said Bernard. "I didn't come down here to go back empty-handed."

"Time is running out for them. Finish up your snack and let's get going" said Michael as he secured his knapsack from the netting and adjusted his canteen.

A few minutes later Mike led his friends along the boulder-strewn, muddy embankment and deep into the subterranean Joppa Cave System. Climbing over the rock-strewn landscape, Michael looked intently for some sign of the missing group. He was not concerned over not finding footprints, for surely the rain-swollen river had risen considerably and had erased any footprints. The only evidence that this passage had been used was the rope ladder. An hour had passed and he was starting to tire. Mike beamed his light to a plateau ahead where they would rest.

As his friends munched on apples and candy bars and talked elatedly about what they had seen, Mike sensed a growing sense of camaraderie developing among them. Even Lydia was playfully beaming her flashlight on the grotesque masks the mud had created on her friends' faces.

Mike got up and walked to a pile of rocks and rubble ten yards away. He played the beam of his light on the rubble-strewn canyon-

74

like walls. Lydia let out a piercing scream as Bernie threw a cave cricket at her.

As Mike turned in the direction of the scream, his flashlight caught a glint of silver wedged in the rubble five yards up into the pile. Disregarding the screaming he raced up the rocks and held up a discarded tuna fish can in his hand.

"Tuna fish! Tuna fish!" he hollered, above Lydia's diminishing scream.

"What?" yelled Bernie.

"I found a tuna fish can" said Michael scavenging among the rocks. He bent and picked up another one. "The kind they sell in those vending machines back at the lodge. We're onto them. They camped out here and threw their garbage among the rocks up here. We have the same kind of tuna fish in our knapsacks."

He came down from the rocks and showed them the cans. " "We've got to get moving. They are a day and a half, almost two days ahead of us. No stopping for the next four hours. There are five people venturing down here for the first time. We're going to move twice as fast as they did. Are you up to it?" asked Mike, hearing the resolve in his voice. A sense of dogged determination to find these people quickened within him.

"Let's do it!" answered Tran, hurrying back to where he had left their packs.

They followed the meandering river. Michael picked up the pace. They were now into a slow trot, bounding over rocks and rubble and an occasional boulder. At times, someone would misstep and fall forward. The others would come running back and assist their fallen friend, urging him or her to hurry up. The fallen youth would say nothing but would run ahead. Sometimes they slowed up a little to admire the beauty and color of a certain stalactite or were mesmerized by the height of the ceiling reaching 60 and 80 feet at certain intervals. Mike felt that their courage was rewarding them with vistas of untold beauty. He especially liked the widening of the river passage. It made the bank easier to run on.

THE STUYVESANT CONNECTION

After twenty minutes, they slowed their pace and picked out a large flat rock to rest on. Hoisting themselves up, they dropped their packs and lay back on them as if they were pillows. They all were breathing heavily. Tran took out his notebook and began to retrace from memory the major turns, unusual formations and obstacles they encountered.

Mike estimated that they had covered a little over a mile and a half and would need as good a map as they could get for the return trip. He wanted to make sure they had a reasonable sense of how far they were from the sinkhole entrance. It was easy right now because they were following the river. If and when they left the river, any maps drawn would have to be accurate, detailing every twist and turn.

After covering another half mile Mike gave out a whoop as he held a candy wrapper and shook it triumphantly. The Stuyvesant kids recognized it as sold in the vending machine back at the lodge. Apparently one of Butch's friends had gotten hungry and quickly disposed of the wrapper as he trekked along the river. The young people quickened their pace, seeming to regain energy with each new discovery. Mike was glad that kids get hungry. Hurrah, for littering, Mike thought" to himself.

The river began to narrow, and the ceiling slowly lowered as the beams of their flashlights began to brighten their compressed surroundings. The beams of their flashlights, once lost in the immensity of the river cavern, now shone brightly against the yellow limestone wall creating shadows. Bernard would stop the group every once and a while and create animal patterns against the limestone wall as Tran acted as lighting director. This brought laughter from the group, and calls for more, but Mike patiently nudged them on, reassuring them that every step was bringing them closer to Butch and his friends.

Tired and hungry, they dropped their packs and collapsed to the ground at a point where the river narrowed to a fifteen-foot stream of roaring, very deep water.

THE STUYVESANT CONNECTION

"Do you get the feeling we're going deeper into the cavern? I mean, I've noticed a definite incline the last half mile or so. I bet we've descended at least a hundred feet" said Mike.

"I know I've noticed a change in the geology of the passage. It's almost as if we're nearing granite bedrock. Look at the wall behind you. That's limestone on top and that grey rock is granite at the bottom. From what I've read, most cave systems in this area are almost exclusively limestone" said Tran as he snapped open a tuna fish can and devoured the contents.

"I hope you know where we are, and how we're going to get back!" said Lydia as she munched on an apple and stared at Mike.

"How can we get lost, Lydia? All you have to do is follow the yellow rock river back to the sinkhole," said Bernard tossing a candy wrapper into the raging water.

"Eh, Bernard, no littering," joked Mike. "Remember what Todd said about leaving these passages just as pristine and natural as we found them. No graffiti and no littering!" with that said he tossed an apple core into the swirling water. A twinge of guilt made him gather the rest of the refuse into a small plastic baggie and he pressed it deeply into his knapsack. His friends followed suit and did the same.

"Let's get moving! We've been down here about five and a half hours. We agreed to search for ten, maybe twelve hours at most. We have to keep up a rapid pace. It's our only chance of finding them," said Mike as he extended a hand to help Lydia to her feet.

For the next twenty minutes, they jogged and walked and climbed over small boulders as they penetrated deeper into the recesses of the Joppa Cave System. The cavern passage continued to compress on itself. Stalactites and stalagmites became smaller. The passage was only fifteen-feet-wide now and occupied almost exclusively by the river. The four had to hug the wall at certain points where the embankment narrowed to one foot. The river was deep and rapid. The water hurtling through the passage was deafening and they had to shout to one another in order to be heard.

THE STUYVESANT CONNECTION

Mike felt increasingly anxious and afraid, both for himself and for the safety of his friends. An accidental fall into the raging water could prove perilous at this point. Mike cursed Butch and his reckless friends for drawing them into this situation. He then felt remorseful, knowing that Butch and his friends must be in dire straits. He didn't want to think of the alternative. Continuing another half mile Mike couldn't believe his eyes when the beam of his flashlight played upon a rock wall. The roaring river disappeared underneath it.

"I think I know what happened here," said Tran. "The spring flooding plugged up this passage. Two days ago, Butch was able to pass through with little trouble. This wall is granite. Over millions of years the water took the path of least resistance and that is the limestone underneath" Tran pointed to the space just above the roaring water.

"Well how are we going to get through? We don't have any submarines handy!" Lydia said looking tired and cynical.

"We have to go back and look for a cut-around," Tran replied. "With the flow of water we have here, there's got to be many cut-arounds branching off the main river."

"I just thought of something," said Mike, trying to recall something he read about in *The Longest Cave*. "People have been in similar situations before. If we are lucky, we will find a small squeeze tube emanating off the main passage. As bad as the spring flooding looks this year, over eons of time, when all Joppa Ridge was underwater, small vein-like tubes eroded their way around the main river. Our job is to find them!"

Casting the beams of their flashlights around the wall, the young people looked for the tubes. Tran and Bernard retreated back a hundred feet and searched that area, slowly moving forward. At one point Tran scaled a small rock ledge and climbed over a rockfall. He started removing fifty-pound boulders and pushing others aside.

"Got something, Tran?" asked Mike.

THE STUYVESANT CONNECTION

"Not yet, just checking," said Tran. "Where there's a rockfall there is often soft rock and a chance to find a tube."

Lydia checked all around the granite wall for an opening. Mike was working his way toward Bernie and Tran. Bernie was busily removing boulders when Tran shouted.

"Got one! It looks pretty good for skinny people," he added.

Shining his light on the hole that Tran had found, Mike chided him for fooling them. Bernie joked about Tran finding a rat hole to Lydia when he saw the size of the opening.

"It's a lot bigger than that," said Tran as he moved several boulders that revealed an opening about eighteen inches in diameter.

"Look, Tran, it's muddy and gooky in there. I'm not going in there. It's probably filled with worms and spiders" said Lydia.

"Tran, maybe we should look for a larger tube. I don't think Bernie and I could fit through there," said Mike.

"Yea you can, all you have to do is imitate an inchworm," said Tran as he disappeared headfirst into the opening pushing his shoulder sack in front of him.

The three young people looked at each other, shrugged their shoulders and set about imitating Tran. "We don't have time to look for a larger opening" said Mike with admiration for Tran's courage. "Lydia, you get behind Bernie. I'll bring up the rear."

Slowly and cautiously they entered the tube. Tran was yelling muffled instructions about the length of the tube passage. Mike became concerned that maybe it was too long. It would be harder to retreat that to go forward. He looked at the opalescent hands on his watch. If they took more than fifteen minutes and hadn't reached the end of it, he would order a retreat so as not to endanger his friends.

The tube was muddy, dank, and cold. A definite breeze was wafting through it, usually a sign of a larger opening ahead. After five minutes Lydia requested a rest. Tran yelled back that the tube was narrowing even more. Oh great, Mike thought to himself, that's all we need for someone to get wedged in a skinny tube.

THE STUYVESANT CONNECTION

Pushing themselves forward, Mike was startled when Bernard began yelling. The tube amplified sound and the yelling was deafening.

"What the hell was that! Something crawled on my hand and scooted across my face! Good thing I had my batting helmet on because I hit my head on the ceiling" said Bernard.

"It was probably a blind cave salamander. They like these dark and muddy places. Don't worry, just keep going" said Mike.

"We've been in this tube for over ten minutes and there is still no end to it," said Lydia as she complained about feeling claustrophobic.

Lydia was right. The passage was getting narrower by the minute. Mike felt his helmet scraping the ceiling more often. "Lydia, everything is going to be O.K. We'll be out of here soon," Mike said in a soothing voice as he tried to reassure her.

Mike checked his watch. Fifteen minutes had elapsed. He hesitated in stopping them. They had gone so far. If they turn back now, it would be the end of everything. Butch and the others would be given up for lost — they had to push on. But if this thing went on endlessly then he and his friends would suffer a worse fate. When Tran yelled back that he had entered a large underground passage, joy and relief pulsed through Mike's body. He had begun to feel like Floyd Collins, who died an agonizing death when he became trapped in Salt Cave in 1927.

The four young people scrambled out of their claustrophobic confines and shook off the accumulated mud and water from their clothes. They played their flashlights off the wall of the spacious passage and marveled at the beauty of the colors nature reflected back at them.

"Nature's gift to the courageous; she reveals herself to those who dare penetrate her secrets," said Mike as he good-naturedly slapped Tran on the back.

THE STUYVESANT CONNECTION

"Look at the orange and green beauty of that rocky ledge over there," said Lydia pointing to the right wall of the passage seventy-five feet away.

"The green comes from traces of copper oxides embedded in the limestone while the orange is from iron oxide traces," Tran said. "I think we should rest here, Mike. I want to do a map survey of what we just came through," Tran dropped his knapsack to the ground.

"Yea, let's do it," Mike said as he rubbed his shoulder muscles and stretched his arms in a yawn. "Feels great just to be able to move freely."

"I don't know about you guys, but my batteries are running low," said Bernie rummaging through his sack for replacements.

"And I'm starving!" said Lydia as she pulled an apple from her sack.

Mike took a drink of water from his canteen and brushed away some loose rocks from a boulder to make a seat for himself. "I was *this close* to ordering a retreat," he said bringing his thumb and forefinger together. "I was afraid the tube went on for miles and that we were going to exhaust ourselves."

"I was thinking the same thing," said Tran. "But there was too much at stake to turn back too soon. I mean you don't know how happy I was to see that opening. I figure we went 400 yards."

"When Bernie yelled, I thought we were finished. When his helmet hit the ceiling, I thought there had been some kind of cave-in up ahead," said Lydia.

The four teenagers laughed and shared their feelings about what they had just gone through. Mike played his flashlight about their surroundings while Tran worked on the survey map. Lydia cut up an apple with a penknife and passed pieces around. Bernard replenished the batteries of each flashlight. A working relationship was developing among them. Mike was touched by the fact that everyone was finding his/her niche and planning ahead for any eventuality.

THE STUYVESANT CONNECTION

Mike got up and walked around. Bernard had replaced the batteries in his flashlight. They had agreed to a ten-minute-rest. He had five minutes to explore and consider the next course of action. This passage has to connect with the river again, he thought to himself. If it doesn't we're in trouble. He walked about fifty yards from the group and returned.

"O.K, everybody up! We got six hours left before we turn back. This thing seems to go on for a long way. We've got to make contact with the river. It's our only chance to find them," said Mike hoisting up his knapsack. "Don't forget to clean up. We don't want rats or blind salamanders," he added jokingly.

THE STUYVESANT CONNECTION

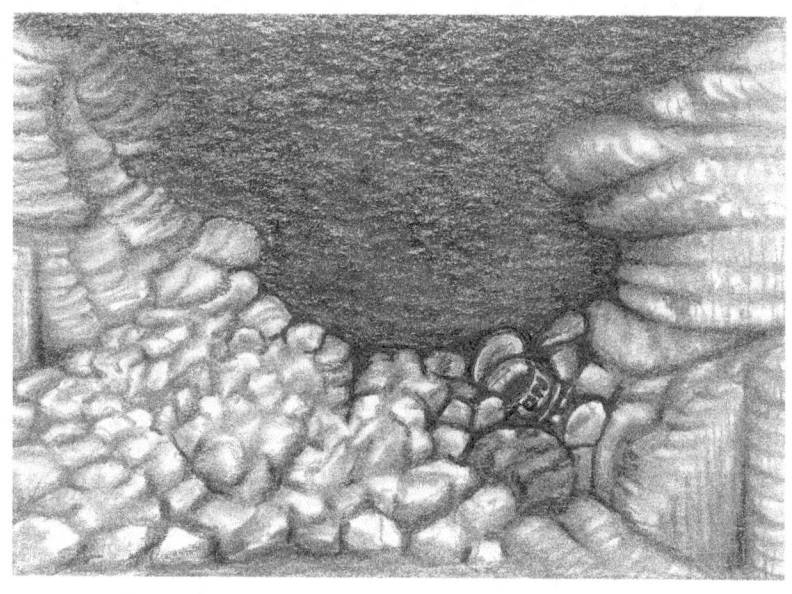

CHAPTER XI

"This is unbelievable," said Bernard as they made their way through narrow, twisting canyons and huge rooms of breakdown. Bernard looked at his friends. They had apparently forgotten the aches and pains of the tube and were mesmerized by the beauty of the orange-white flow stone that surrounded them on all sides. They had been walking down this passage for a half hour and still no end was in sight. They stopped to admire some gypsum flowers that Tran pointed out. He told them this was a very dry passage. Mike looked disappointed and worried.

Bernard adjusted the ropes encircling his right shoulder. They were starting to cause an irritation so he switched them to his left shoulder. The passage was as wide as an avenue and one's voice resonated beautifully, so Bernard began to sing:

"I started on a trek one day to find some friends who had lost their way.

I knew we had to find them soon, because the water was raging from a spring monsoon.

So, Mike and I and Lydia and Tran crawled and crept and carried on.

We fought back fears until we found Butch, Laurie, Tony, Carol and Jon."

"This story has an ending that we haven't reached yet," said Mike in a higher pitch. "Listen, in the distance," he added, picking up Bernard's cadence, "a sound we can't forget!"

They stopped; Bernard heard the low but distinct sound of flowing water gurgling in the distance.

"It's water, man. We gotta go. I just love listening to that flow," said Bernard as he raced past his friends and hopped over breakdown. His friends raced after the dancing receding light. As it grew dimmer, they picked up their speed. After a while the light disappeared as the roar of the water grew to a crescendo. Bernard was kneeling on a pebbly bank; splashing water on his face. His flashlight cast an eerie reflection on the water's surface. Light reflected and rippled off the opposite wall, giving added life to the discovery.

"Wow, this is neat. All we need is a raft to navigate this thing" said Bernard taking in the width of the river. It was about 20-feet-across. The spring rain had swollen the river and left only a bank for walkers to negotiate. Ahead was only a black hole which roaring water disappeared into.

The group rested for five minutes before making their way along the damp, rocky bank. Bernard took the lead while Mike brought up the rear. The bank was slippery from fungi and mosses brought in by the river. At times the group had to hug the wall. The water seemed to be steadily rising as the passage was getting smaller. Bernard cut a small piece of nylon rope which he passed to Michael who was now taking the lead. They used it as a safety line with Bernard and Michael keeping it taut so that Lydia and Tran would be kept close to the wall. Bernard kept up encouraging chatter as he tried to distract them from the precarious position they were in. The embankment was turning into an ascending ledge so that they were now ten feet above the water line.

Suddenly Lydia lost her footing as the accumulated moss on the ledge caused her left foot to slip outward. She twisted around and tried to grab for the line. She screamed for help. The line held momentarily, then gave way as the weight of her body pulled the safety line from their hands. She plummeted face first into the cold raging water and was swept away toward the gaping darkness ahead. Her three friends reacted in disbelief. Bernie was paralyzed with fear as the current pulled her to and fro. Michael yelled for her not to lose her flashlight. Just before she disappeared into the blackness ahead, she feebly raised her hand. Her screams were lost in the roaring cacophony of water being sucked into the black hole ahead.

THE STUYVESANT CONNECTION

Bernie knew what they had to do. Moving fast along the precarious ledge, they came to a point where the ledge descended and approached the bank of the river again. The passage narrowed considerably until there was almost no bank at all, only water pouring into a gaping black hole. The boys looked at each other, not wanting to talk about what they thought.

"We're going to hook up a pulley system and we gotta do it fast. I don't know what's in there or how long it goes. Mike, get your rubber suit on. Try to keep as warm as you can. You are going in after her. Hopefully, she is hanging on to something. I don't want to think about the alternative. Tran, you're going to have to help me retrieve them. We're fighting against a current, so it won't be easy. Mike, take the harness with you. If you find Lydia, strap it on her and we'll bring her back. Mike, I think we gotta think about returning. We may have lost her," said Bernard eyes downcast, as he adjusted a knot to loop over Michael.

"We'll find her," whispered Michael slipping into the knotted loop.

"Yea, we'll find her," Tran said in a worried, unconvincing tone.

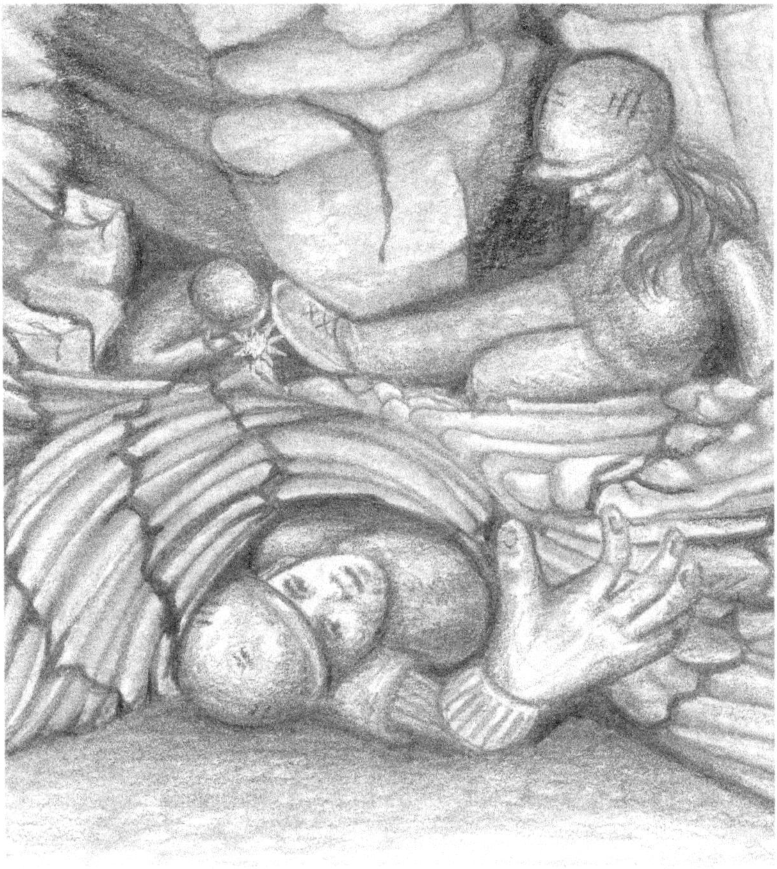

CHAPTER XII

Michael made the sign of the cross, said a prayer to himself, and plunged into the cold raging water. Bernie and Tran played out the line slowly at first as not to let the current dictate Mike's progress. Michael felt the water seeping into the rubber suit. The chill caused him to shiver. Poor Lydia, Mike thought to himself. She had warned them about taking stupid chances. She was the sun of our group, earthbound, protective, not caught up in macho posturing — trying to save the world. It was enough just being around friends. "Don't put other people in danger," she had warned. Mike felt guilty about convincing the others to undertake such a stupid risk.

The river began to widen as Mike progressed forward. Mike's light now lit up a greater area. Treading water and swimming ahead were difficult. His feet felt leaden but the air spaces in the rubber suit kept him afloat. At times, he tugged at the line. They were letting it out too slowly. Thinking of my safety, huh. Well, I didn't think much of Lydia's safety and now she's gone. He cursed to himself and tears came to his eyes as he swam forward. Pulling on the line, he yelled to try to reach Lydia.

He pushed deeper into the passage. The line was now extending 250 feet into the passage. Yelling out Lydia's name and crying at the same time, he was now pure emotion, thrashing forward into the subterranean blackness of an ancient cave system.

"Lydia, I love you! I'm so sorry! Do you hear me? I love you, Lydia!"

"I love you too, Michael," came the feeble reply from up ahead. It was now joined by a chorus of loud and boisterous voices.

"Michael, we love you! Michael, we love you! Michael, we love you!" Then a single masculine voice broke the darkness. "Now get us the hell out of here!"

THE STUYVESANT CONNECTION

In all his life, Mike had never been so happy as he was at this instant. All his dreams were coming true. Lydia was still alive. Butch and his friends had been found. The risk had all been worth it. Treading water 400 feet underground in a cold, dark cave passage, Mike experienced the singular joy that can only come to those who have saved the life of another human being.

He still could not see the loud and boisterous voices emanating from up ahead but the music of their cries gave incredible strength to his body. He tugged at the line excitedly to tell Bernie and Tran that something great had happened and stroked through the water.

The voices were reverberating throughout the passage. Fifty feet ahead he saw the dim faint outline of a flashlight being waved excitedly. His body was getting numb from the cold water. Tugging again at the line, he swam forward to the throng of encouraging voices. He could now see a number of people jumping up and down and Lydia wrapped in a blanket waving as she leaned against the rock wall.

Kicking furiously, he made it to the ledge. A throng of arms lifted him from the water. Butch's muddy face broke into a wide grin. "You did it, guy! I thought we were lost forever. When we pulled in Lydia, you'll never know what it did for our spirit. We'd given up all hope of ever being found."

"Here, get out of those wet clothes" said a brown-haired girl as she removed the wet suit from his body.

"I got no feeling in my legs," said Michael.

"Don't worry, Michael. It'll come back," said Lydia still shivering in her blanket. She reached up and embraced him with one hand as he knelt over to talk to her. Cheek held tightly to cheek, they stayed that way until they could feel each other's warmth. "Everything's O.K. now," she whispered. "We found them." Looking up at a boy named Tony draped in a blanket she waved and said, "And they found us."

"Seeing Lydia float by was the sweetest sight. We've been marooned on this ledge for two days now. We only had this dim flashlight and a few candy bars left when you guys came by," said Tony as he knelt down near a girl who was quiet and withdrawn. "Carol, we have visitors. Everything is gonna be O.K," said Tony as he stroked her hair.

"Going to be all right, Tony? You promise, you promise, Tony?" said Carol with a vacant stare.

"Carol, look who's here. We got company. This is Lydia and this is Mike. Mike brought a line with him. We're getting outta here. We're gonna see the sun again and feel the wind on our face. We're going home!" said Tony still stroking her hair.

She smiled at Lydia and Mike and then started to cry. Tony held her.

"Butch, what made you get into this mess? Why didn't you tell somebody where you were going? You know they've got the whole place mobilized looking for you and your friends," said Michael.

"My father's an amateur spelunker. He was exploring the Joppa Cave System when he was stationed at an Air Force base nearby years ago. I came across some old maps he had made, after me and my friends had won the science essay at our school. I convinced them to come along with me. It was stupid. I told them we'd turn back but then we got stuck on this bank because the river kept rising" said Butch, eyes downcast, his right hand peeling mud from his arm. "I screwed up and almost lost my friends."

He looked around at Tony, Laurie, Jon, and Carol and his eyes welled up as if they were silently asking forgiveness.

"How did you know we were trying to make a connection to Mammoth?" asked Jon, a tall blond boy who was holding the safety line tightly with both hands.

"When I first met you guys on the train, you were talking about doing a little side exploring on your own. You all hushed up when someone mentioned Joppa Ridge. It didn't dawn on me that you were trying to make a connection until I saw Joppa Ridge from the lodge dining room. Then everything fell into place. I had been reading about the numerous attempts to connect Joppa Ridge to

THE STUYVESANT CONNECTION

Mammoth. They always resulted in failure. I had a feeling Butch was reckless enough to try. I didn't know you had some maps. Did you chart new territory?" asked Michael.

"No, my dad went even further, about two miles more. Then he came to a rockfall and had to turn back. So much for connection." said Butch trailing off. "The only connection made around here is the Stuyvesant connection in finding us. Thanks for caring enough to follow up a hunch." Butch extended his hand to shake Michael's and then Lydia's.

"It's the only connection that counts," said Michael looking around at each person and nodding recognition of their thanks.

"Your friends are tugging on the line, Mike. How should we respond?" asked Jon.

"Just give three sharp tugs. That'll let them know we are loading up," said Michael regaining a sense of command. "Jon, I think you should go first. When you get to Bernie and Tran, tell them I'm sending Carol next with Tony as an escort."

"Mike! Look, somebody's coming!" said Lydia, excitedly pointing upstream.

Mike turned and saw a bright, blinding light as if from arc lamps lighting up the horizon several hundred feet away. It was bobbing up and down as it lit the once hidden subterranean beauty of their surroundings. As it drew closer he felt as if a Hollywood production was being filmed. Bernie called out to Mike and Lydia as he waved frantically from a pontoon raft.

"The National Park Service to the rescue! Everybody O.K?" asked Bernie as he manually counted heads from the raft, now twenty-five feet away.

"We did it! Bernie. We made a connection. We found them!" said Michael with a raised clenched fist.

"Awright!" said Bernie happily pounding the side of the massive pontoon as it gently drew near the ledge.

THE STUYVESANT CONNECTION

CHAPTER XIII

Michael woke to a gentle rapping on the sturdy oak doors of the lodge bedroom. He looked at the wall clock. It was 10:45 am. He had been asleep for over eleven hours. The return trip through Joppa Ridge had made him bone-weary. Bernard and Tran were still in a deep sleep as Michael walked to the door to open it. A letter had been slipped through at the base of the door. It was addressed to him. He immediately saw that it was from his mother but the return address was unfamiliar. Anxiously opening it, he read:

Dear Michael,

I left your father yesterday because I could no longer stand the abuse. It's something I've been working on for a while now. Father O'Conner has helped me get an apartment on Webb Ave in the Bronx and a job at the Kingsbridge Nursing Home. Right now, I'm only an aide but if I study, I can become a Practical Nurse. The hours allow me to work and be back when the kids get home from school. They will have to commute by subway for a few months until they get a transfer. Your father will have to work out his own destiny and decide what's important. I've found a new self-respect these last few days that I want to build on. Lots to tell you when you get home. Your brothers are proud you won the Science award and can't wait to hear about your adventure in Kentucky. You're going away for a while has showed me that you can grow even in the most difficult of circumstances. I read somewhere that maturity means tolerating all the ambiguity that there is in life. Well I'm going through that now, dealing with the pain and guilt you sometimes feel in growing, but it's worth it. There's a new chapter being written in the Ryan family and I have a feeling it can only get better.

Love,

your Mother, Anne

P.S. Call Father O'Conner for directions to our new apartment when you get home.

Tears streamed down Michael's face as he folded the letter and placed it in his wallet. Somehow his mother had found the strength to do what had to be done. He felt for his father but feelings of contempt and anger overwhelmed the sympathetic ones. Wow, he said to himself as he brushed away the tears. This has been some week, so many things happening all at once — people finding courage to do what has to be done. He sucked in his breath to stifle all the emotion he felt as he heard Bernard asking what time it was.

"Time to get up, guys! It's almost 11 am. We got a lot of questions to answer at the luncheon in the lodge dining room. They say reporters from all over the area will be there. Hey, Tran, rise and shine," Michael said as he tossed a pillow that landed squarely at his head.

Tran awoke, still looking groggy from the trip through Joppa Ridge. He massaged his arms, still sore from crawling in a cramped position. He heaved a pillow back at Michael but it fell short. "Man, I had enough of wild caving to last a lifetime." He stood up yawned and stretched his arms. "Feels good to breathe free, see the sun, and just stretch!"

"How's it feel to be a celebrity, Tran? We've got a luncheon to attend at one o'clock. We'll be peppered with questions. Boy, is this gonna make a good report when we get home. Mr. Rubin wanted a report. Well, he gonna get a good one, newspaper clippings, photographs, and all," Michael said.

"Good, that'll save on the writing," said Bernard.

Michael finished dressing and went down the hall to get Lydia. He rapped lightly on the door. She opened it. A broad smile radiated from her face. The white sweater she was wearing accentuated the natural beauty of her features. Michael had never felt so alive and responsive to another person as he felt whenever he was around Lydia. He felt good about himself and the world was full of wondrous possibilities. "I thought we'd all go for a walk before we meet the press at one," said Michael, gazing at her face.

"You know, Michael, my roommate says they're going to name a passage in Joppa Ridge the Stuyvesant Way in celebration of the rescue of Butch and his friends. Isn't that great?"

"You know you look beautiful today, Lydia."

"Thank you, Michael. It felt so good just to take a shower. I must have stayed in there ten minutes. I never realized how cold I was down there in Joppa Ridge." She smiled at him.

Walking down the corridor to meet Bernie and Tran, Michael hesitantly grasped Lydia's hand. He started to withdraw it, expecting rejection when she grasped it tightly and enveloped it into her own palm.

Michael beamed as he saw Bernie and Tran step into the hallway.